Dinah's Dilemma

By Linda Shenton Matchett

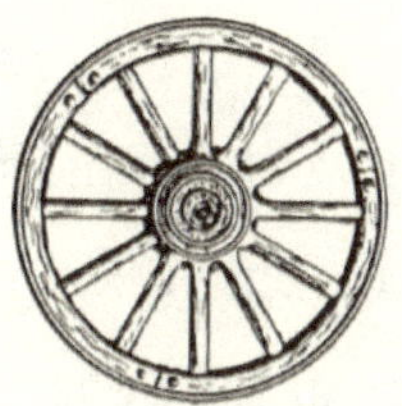

Chapter One

Nathan Childs raced across the field toward his daughter as she toddled with determination toward the fire. How had he managed to let Florence get so far from his side? The three-year-old was fearless, and he knew better than to give her too much freedom. He'd already prevented her from crawling under the fence into the horse pen and trying to climb one of the massive sugar maples that sheltered the food tables at the town's Memorial Day celebration.

Perspiration trickled down his spine, and his shirt clung to his back as the midday sun beat down on his head and glared into his eyes. The morning had dawned unseasonably warm, and the temperatures continued to rise. Summers in Nebraska were known as scorchers, but May was early to be fighting heat and humidity.

"Florence," he shouted as he ran to gain the child's attention, but his voice was swallowed up in the myriad conversations, music, and laughter of Lincoln's citizens. Nebraska's capital had exploded in population over the last eighteen months, and Burlington and Missouri

River Railroad's first train was due at the end of June. Sure to bring even more people. Not what he'd envisioned when he moved West after Georgianna's death.

Finally, close enough to grab her, he scooped Florence into his arms and pressed her close to his chest, her small body warm and soft. "What were you thinking, baby girl? Fire is bad. You need to be more careful and stay near me."

"No!" She arched her back and flailed her legs. "Fire is pretty, Daddy." Her face reddened, and she sobbed as if she'd lost her best friend. Tears dampened her cheeks, her blue eyes swimming.

His heart dropped. He hated when she cried. Her sobs made him feel as helpless as a newborn calf. He never knew what to do when she got like this. He hugged her closer and rubbed circles on her back in an effort to calm her.

"Sounds like someone's tired."

Nathan turned and nodded.

His best friend and the town sheriff, Alfred Denard, approached, a wide grin creasing his face below his black Stetson hat. "How about if you take a break and let Livvy watch her for a while. Looks like you both could use a change of scenery."

"Is it that obvious?"

Alfred chuckled as they headed for the cluster of women seated under the trees. "Sometimes I think you'd rather face the Mes Gang or Farrington Brothers than a crying little girl."

Nathan shrugged. "At least when I was chasing outlaws as a Pinkerton, I'd been trained and knew what to expect. Raising Florence is another whole ball of wax. Every day is different, so something I learned yesterday, doesn't necessarily work today." He blew out a deep breath as Florence quieted and tucked her thumb into her mouth. "I love her with my whole being, but maybe I should have let Georgianna's parents take her. I'm failing miserably."

"Do you think living with her grandparents is what's best for her?"

Nearing the blanket where Alfred's wife, Olivia, sat, Nathan paused and grimaced. "I don't know anymore. The thought of having to decide paralyzes me."

Livvy rose and held out her arms, her blonde hair swept into a tight bun at the base of her neck. She smiled, and her face glowed. "Are you going to let me spend time with your sweet little girl, Nathan? I've been aching to hold that child all day."

Florence chortled and reached for the buxom young woman. Nathan transferred his daughter into her waiting embrace, and his arms felt bereft. He shoved his hands into his pockets.

"Can I keep her through dinner, Nathan?" Livvy poked Florence's belly then rubbed noses with the giggling youngster. "We'll have lots of fun together, won't we?"

"You sure that's not too much time, Livvy?"

She shook her head. "Not enough, if you ask me." She jerked her head toward the corrals. "You boys head over to the pens and enjoy yourselves. The roping competitions should be starting soon."

Alfred ran his finger along her jaw then kissed her cheek, a starry-eyed look on his face. Married for three years, he still mooned over his wife, like a besotted schoolboy. Livvy had come from Atlanta as his friend's mail-order bride. Claiming love at first sight, they'd married immediately. "You holler if you need help, honey."

"I'll be fine." She winked at her husband. "Now, scoot."

Nathan pressed his lips together as his heart tugged. It had been too long since anyone looked at him like Livvy gazed at Alfred, but he had enough going on without saddling himself with a wife. He turned toward the festivities.

He couldn't ask for better friends than Alfred and Livvy. Two days after he'd arrived fifteen months ago, they'd shown up at his claim with food and friendship. Between the two of them, they'd arranged for some of the locals to transport his supplies from Omaha then pulled together a cadre of men to help build the house and barn. Livvy kept him fed when he didn't feel like eating in those early days of mourning after Georgianna's death. He'd figured moving to a new location would lessen the hollow feeling in his heart since she'd never lived in Nebraska, but his grief had followed him.

A city girl born and bred, she would have hated life on the plains, but he still missed her presence. Especially in the small things. Rustling up a stack of pancakes or sitting on the front porch watching the sun dip behind the trees, talking about everything and nothing.

The first year in Lincoln had been difficult, but rewarding. The crop had been decent, and he'd put aside some money for the future. Maybe to purchase the adjoining plot. Too soon to do so, but the idea was tempting. This year's wheat had done well and would be ready to harvest in another couple of months.

A stiff gust kicked up dust from the animal enclosures and swirled above the beasts. The acrid smell of manure clung to the breeze as it lifted his hat. Would he ever get used to the constant wind?

"All right, gents, time to see who's the best roper in the Lincoln." Barnard Johnson, a cattle rancher who owned the largest spread outside of town, stood in the center of one of the corrals, thumbs tucked in the waistband of his denim pants. A pair of ivory-handled pistols, Colts, if Nathan wasn't mistaken, hung from an ornate holster around his substantial belly. His boots gleamed.

Alfred jabbed Nathan with a sharp elbow. "You should take a turn. Show up the rest of the boys."

"No, thanks. I want to make friends not enemies."

"This is just a friendly competition."

"I'll pass, but you should take a turn. Confirm why you're the best sheriff in Nebraska."

"Because I can lasso the outlaws?" Alfred's chuckle rumbled in his chest. "Think I'll pass, too."

"Hey, Nathan. Aren't you going to show off those muscles of yours?"

Nathan cringed at the sound of Katrina Wainwright's strident voice that could send dogs and bats running for cover. She'd made her intentions clear at Christmas that he was the man for her despite his protestations to the contrary. Not one to be put off easily, she turned up at his side every chance she got. He squared his shoulders and pivoted on his heel.

Dipping his head in greeting, he forced a smile. "Good afternoon, Miss Wainwright. Are you enjoying today's event?"

Her giggle ended with a snort as she slapped his arm. "Katrina. How many times do I have to remind you to call me by my given name?"

"It wouldn't be proper, Miss Wainwright."

"We're not exactly in a Boston drawing room."

"True—"

"Hey, Katrina, watch this!" From inside the corral, one of Mr. Johnson's cowhands waved his hands over his head.

She turned, and Nathan took the opportunity to escape. Alfred followed close behind him. They strode to the six-foot tables piled with platters of food, grabbed a couple of plates, and chose several delicious-looking items. Nathan frowned. "That was a close one, but I feel bad for sneaking away."

"Don't. You've made it clear you're not interested. And after the incident with Florence when she took the child from the church nursery without your permission, she ought to know you'll never trust her." Alfred held an oatmeal cookie up to his nose and took a deep breath. "I do love my wife's baking." He took a bite and grinned. Shoving the rest of the treat into his mouth, he clapped Nathan on the back as he finished chewing. "I know how you can get rid of her."

Nathan narrowed his eyes. "I'm afraid to ask."

"Don't be. I have the perfect solution. You need a substitute girlfriend, and I know where you can get one."

"No. Before you say anything else, the answer is no. I'm not going to apply for a mail-order bride." Tears pricked the backs of his eyes. "You and Livvy are very happy, but I'm not in the market for a wife, and I don't think I'll ever be." He swallowed against the lump that had formed in his throat.

"I understand your grief. Don't forget I lost my first wife six years ago. But you can find love again. Unfortunately, the ratio of women to men out here isn't good, and your choices in Lincoln are limited." He wiggled his eyebrows. "Unless, you'd like to reconsider Miss Wainwright."

"Absolutely not." Nathan shuddered. "Despite her outward beauty, she's deceitful, and I could never love a woman like that. Florence and I are doing just fine with the two of us."

"Are you so sure about that? Your little girl needs a mother. You're not being fair to Florence. Please think about contacting Milly Crenshaw at the Westward Home and Hearts Matrimonial Agency." He squeezed Nathan's shoulder. "Now, as much as I enjoy time with you, I'm going to sit with my beautiful wife."

Nathan watched him leave, a jaunty air in his step as he threaded his way through the crowd to Livvy. She beamed as he approached then blushed after he bent and whispered something in her ear.

Was Alfred right? Could he find a woman he would love as he had Georgianna? He surveyed the townspeople, his gaze stopping to rest on Katrina. Full figured with a peaches-and-cream complexion, she had ebony-colored hair and deep-brown eyes. A gorgeous woman evidenced by the number of young men crowding around her like a flock of chicks.

But he couldn't get past her subterfuge. Plain and simple, she'd lied then claimed the whole thing was a misunderstanding. Should he try to find an honest woman who would love Florence as her own? Did this Milly Crenshaw have the answer? Surely, anyone she sent couldn't be any worse than Katrina.

June 1, 1870
Baltimore, Maryland

Chapter Two

Dinah Simpkins fought the urge to skip down the sidewalk on her way to the post office. Surely, the letter from Ellicott City offering her the teaching position had arrived by now. During the nerve-wracking interview, town officials seemed impressed with her education and ideas. How long did it take to make the decision?

Sunlight broke through the clouds as if they were also celebrating her new job. She smiled and straightened her spine. Compared to Baltimore, Ellicott City was a tiny spot on the map, but the opportunity to take charge of her own schoolhouse was a dream come true.

She'd welcome the youngsters each morning with a smile and perhaps a snack. A mix of students from farm families and millworkers would create a challenge, but she was up to the task. The school building had all the modern conveniences, with each child receiving his or her own slate. Unlike many other small towns, Ellicott City's schoolhouse didn't double as the church.

Older children would bring in the coal to heat the building, and younger students would clean up after classes were done at three o'clock. Field trips and outdoor activities would round out their education.

Increasing her pace, she slipped past a man and woman sauntering along the pavement. Engrossed in each other, they barely acknowledged her. Her heart stuttered. Too bad she would never marry. Life might be easier with a husband by her side, but no man in his right mind would take on her family's woes.

Perspiration trickled between her shoulder blades as Baltimore's typical humidity engulfed the city. Those with money had already fled to their cooler summer residences. The remaining residents would make do until the temperatures broke sometime in September. With any luck, she'd be able to relocate well before the beginning of school.

The brick post office came into view, and Dinah's smile widened. Today was going to change her life. Of that she was sure.

Dinah retied the ribbons on her hat then lifted her skirts and climbed the stairs. As she reached the top, her best friend, Vera Edgecomb, burst out the door clutching a thick envelope. Topped with a straw hat, her voluminous ash-blonde hair hung in sausage curls. Her green eyes sparkled. "Dinah, I'm so glad I've run into you. I just received the most exciting news!"

"I'm expecting a letter myself."

"Then we must go inside and collect your mail." Vera linked arms with her. "We can share our announcements together."

Dinah's Dilemma

Heart pounding, Dinah peeked through the tiny window in the box assigned to her family. A single envelope. Her breath hitched as she slid the key into the lock and opened the door. With trembling fingers, she withdrew the missive, and her eyes widened. Stark against the cream-colored paper, the address of Ellicott City Town Hall was emblazoned on the upper-left corner. She pressed the envelope to her chest and closed her eyes.

Vera nudged her shoulder. "Don't make me wait! Open your letter, then we can take turns sharing our announcements."

Dinah's eyes flew open, and her face warmed. "Sorry. I feel like I've been waiting forever, although my interview was only two weeks ago." She slid her finger under the flap then pulled out the single sheet of paper. Her gaze raced down the page, and her stomach plummeted. The town had chosen another candidate. Her shoulders slumped, and she pressed her lips together to keep them from quivering.

"Distressing news?" Vera's voice was soft and filled with dread.

"I didn't get the teaching job as expected. Now, I won't be able to help with the family finances, and we'll probably lose the house." Tears trickled down Dinah's cheeks. "But the worst of it is their decision isn't based on my capabilities. They found out about my stepfather's gambling problems and my brothers' association with the Bloody Tubs gang, and don't want a teacher with a soiled reputation."

"Oh, honey. I'm so sorry." Vera patted her arm. "Perhaps you should apply for jobs farther from home. Somewhere no one knows the name Simpkins."

"But my real name isn't Simpkins. I use it to avoid confusion, but Chester never adopted me. My last name is Reinhardt, and that's what I used to apply for the job." She pulled a handkerchief from her reticule and wiped her eyes. "How did they discover my identity?"

"Good question, but perhaps the rejection is for the best. It might not feel like it right now, but God must have different plans for you."

"Does He even care about me, Vera? My brothers are criminals, and my stepfather is going to debtors' prison if he can't come up with the money he owes."

"Half brothers."

"What does it matter? We're still related if only through Mama." Dinah dabbed at her cheeks and took a deep breath. "I'm sorry for breaking down. You haven't had a chance to tell me your news."

"Your feelings are more important right now."

"And I'd feel better if we could share your good fortune. Tell me what's in your letter."

Vera's face pinked, and she grinned. "I'm getting married."

"What?" Dinah gaped at her friend. "I didn't think you were seeing anyone."

"I'm not. Well, at least not here. I answered an advertisement for a mail-order bride in Wyoming. We've been corresponding for months, and he's proposed." She waved the envelope. "There's money and a train ticket for me. I leave on Saturday."

"So soon? Why didn't you say anything to me?"

"I don't know. First, I was embarrassed. I've not met anyone who has done this. Then I was afraid it might not work out."

Dinah embraced Vera and sniffled. "I'm happy for you and hope you'll let me help you prepare for your trip. And you must write often, so I can hear about your new adventure."

"I will." Her eyes lit. "You should apply to be a mail-order bride. You could get out from under Chester's reputation."

"Thanks for the suggestion, but I'll think of another solution. No man should have to take on my family's problems." She forced a smile and looped her arm through Vera's. "Now, we should head to your place and get packing."

They hurried from the building and joined the throng of pedestrians on the sidewalk. Pushed and shoved from all sides, Dinah pulled Vera closer. "These crowds seem worse than usual. Where is everyone going?"

"Let's grab that trolley. It's too hot to fight the crush of people in this heat."

With a nod, Dinah looked both ways then followed Vera across the street. Moisture formed at her hairline as she waited in line to board the horse-drawn vehicle. In operation since 1859, Baltimore's extensive trolley system owned over one hundred passenger cars and several hundred horses. Sitting rather than walking the dozen or so blocks to Vera's home would be a lovely change, since she rarely splurged the three-cent fare.

Shoved from behind, she fell to the ground, her hands and knees hitting the pavement. Palms scraped and bleeding, she attempted to climb to her feet when she was kicked in the ribs. Rolling into a ball, she wrapped her arms around her curled legs. Pain shot through her side.

"I know who you are." A short, dark-haired man shook his fist at her. "I'm gonna hurt you like your brothers did to mine."

Shouts rang out, and two men grabbed her assailant, who continued to berate her. "Unhand me. She deserves to be crippled."

Vera dropped beside her then brushed her tangled hair from her face. "Dinah. Are you all right?"

Dinah groaned and sat up, her ribs throbbing. "I think so, but who is he?"

A police officer appeared. "What's the meaning of this?"

The crowd spoke as one, and he held up his hands and whistled. "One at a time." He pointed to the men still restraining her attacker. "Tell me."

"He pushed this young lady down and kicked her. He's been yelling that she deserves what happened to his brother."

The officer glared at the prisoner. "Is this true?"

Face dark, the captive nodded. "Her brothers are part of the Bloody Tubs gang, and they robbed a bank where my brother works. Crippled him with a shot. They deserve payback, and I'm gonna see that she gets it."

"You're going to jail, mister. Hold on to him." He knelt in front of Dinah, concern creasing his forehead. "Are you okay, miss? I could call a doctor."

"No, I'll be fine."

"Are you sure? At least let me help you over to that hotel where you can rest in the lobby."

"Thank you. That would be lovely." Catching her lower lip between her teeth to keep from crying out, Dinah tucked her hand in the bend of the policeman's elbow and leaned on Vera, who'd wrapped her arm around Dinah's waist. Several painful minutes later, she sat on one of the overstuffed sofas in the Crescent Hotel's elegant lobby. She closed her eyes and leaned back. Could this day get any worse?

Vera sat next to her. "I've ordered some tea."

"Thanks, but I don't think a hot beverage is going to solve my problem." She blew out a deep breath. "What am I going to do, Vera? If that man's behavior is any indication, it's not safe for me to remain in Baltimore."

"Now, are you willing to consider being a mail-order bride?" Vera cocked her head. "Heading west will get you out of the city, and being married will give you protection."

"I don't know—"

"Pardon me. I'm sorry to interrupt; however, I couldn't help but overhear your conversation, and I may be able to help you." A petite, pleasingly plump woman attired in the latest fashions smiled brightly. Her honey-colored hair was coiffed and curled. "My name is Mrs. Milly Crenshaw, and this is my secretary and traveling companion, Miss Wadsworth. I own the Westward Home and Hearts Matrimonial Agency."

Dinah's eyes widened, and she glanced at Vera whose eyes twinkled in merriment. "Did you know about this?"

"No." She laughed. "Others might call this a coincidence, but I believe God has intervened to provide your solution." She turned to the two women. "It's wonderful to meet you. I'm Vera Edgecomb, and this is my friend, Dinah Reinhardt."

"May I sit down?" Mrs. Crenshaw gestured toward a nearby settee.

"Absolutely. Please forgive my manners." Dinah's voice quavered. "It's been a difficult day."

"No need to apologize, honey. Tell me about your problem, and we'll see if I can't help you."

Dinah took a deep breath and told the woman about her stepfather's gambling issues and her younger brothers' crimes. Words tumbled out as she shared her hope to teach school and the rejection she'd received, followed by the attack she'd suffered in retribution for her brothers' activities. Finally, she fell silent, and her heart felt lighter than it had in months.

Mrs. Crenshaw patted her knee. "Thank you for your honesty. You're in a tough spot, to be sure, but I believe I have the answer you seek. There is a young man in Nebraska who is looking for a wife. He has a three-year-old daughter who needs a mother. Time is of the essence for him, and it appears to be for you as well. His name is Nathan Childs, and he comes with stellar credentials. If amenable to you, I can put you on a train as soon as you feel well enough to travel."

Face tight, Miss Wadsworth leaned close to Mrs. Crenshaw. "Don't you think we should perform a background check in light of Miss Reinhardt's situation?"

"No, I believe God is leading me to help this young woman."

"This is all so sudden." Dinah plucked at her skirts. Was God sending her to Nebraska? It had been so long since she'd prayed. Why would He intervene in her life and send Mrs. Crenshaw?

"I understand, my dear." Mrs. Crenshaw rose and beckoned to Miss Wadsworth. "I'm staying in the hotel through Monday then return to Boston. You may give me your answer any time prior to then, and I'll make the appropriate arrangements. Meanwhile, I'll be praying for you."

"I've already made my decision." Dinah pushed herself to her feet and held out her hand. "I'll go to Nebraska and marry Mr. Childs."

A cherubic look on her face, Mrs. Crenshaw shook Dinah's hand then pulled her into a warm embrace. She released her with a smile. "You won't be sorry. Rest assured you'll be safe with him. He was a Pinkerton agent for many years. If anyone can keep you from harm, it's Mr. Childs."

Dinah froze. A lawman? Surely, he'd reject her as soon as he discovered her identity.

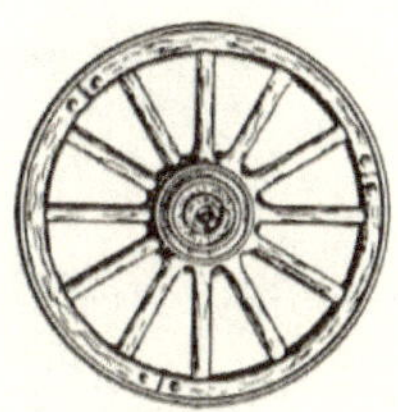

Chapter Three

Hot, dusty air blew through the train's window, and Dinah shifted in her seat. After reading the same paragraph in Jane Austen's *Persuasion* three times, she gave up and closed the book. One of her favorites, the novel failed to assuage her jangled nerves. She checked the watch pinned to her bodice. One more hour, and she'd arrive at her destination where she would begin the next chapter of her life.

Too bad she couldn't write the scenes herself. She'd ensure a happily ever after ending. With a sigh, she tucked the book into her satchel and stared through the glass panes at the vast fields of wheat and corn that stretched to the horizon. Once they'd passed the Allegheny Mountains, the scenery had changed from rolling hills to flat expanses of land. Towns and cities broke up the monotony, but the farther west they traveled, the fewer population centers appeared.

Did Mrs. Crenshaw send the telegram as promised? Had Mr. Childs received it? What would he think of her? Unlike Vera, she was plain-looking and unable to hold a candle to her friend's ash-blonde hair, sparkling blue eyes, and heart-shaped face. Boys stood in line to spend time with Vera, whereas Dinah was often ignored. Why did men have to put such stock in beauty? Didn't they care about a person's behavior and attitude?

She dug into her bag and withdrew a lace-edged handkerchief. Mopping the perspiration from her face and neck, she frowned. Mrs. Crenshaw had told her a bit about Nebraska, but she'd failed to mention the weather. The humidity seemed just as high as Baltimore's. What would winters be like? Would she still be in Lincoln at that time? Surely, Mr. Child's would reject her once he found out about her brothers.

From the rear of the car, a small child babbled. What would it be like to care for a three-year-old? None of her friends had babies, and the youngest student she'd taught in school was six years old. What did one do with a toddler? There had been no time to talk with Mother other than to explain the attack and inform her of the plan to flee West. A few precious moments had been spared for tears, then the remaining time used to pack Dinah's trunks.

Soft weeping sounded, and Dinah turned. A young woman cried into a crumpled hanky. Beside her, a gray-haired woman patted her shoulder and murmured, "You have nothing to be ashamed of, dearie. Leaving him was the right decision."

"But I promised to marry him when I answered the advertisement."

"And he promised to be a kind and faithful husband, not drunk and abusive. Thank the good Lord, his real self was exposed before you wed.

Not all mail-order brides marry their prospective grooms for one reason or another. You'll have another chance to find love."

Dinah's heart hammered in her chest. The possibility that her prospective husband could be a bully never entered her mind. How much had the young woman endured before fleeing? Mrs. Crenshaw claimed Mr. Childs had an unblemished character, but how well did the widow know the man? Would a background check unearth mean-spirited behavior? Especially since he was a Pinkerton agent. Would the organization have the ability to hide his faults?

A shudder snaked up her spine, and she wrapped her arms around her middle. *Please, Lord, keep me safe from harm. If this is Your will, please pave the way for me to trust this man. Help me to be a good wife and mother.*

Time passed. The train slowed, bumping and swaying on the tracks. Brakes squealed, and coal-scented smoke engulfed the wooden platform as they approached. The small wooden station painted burgundy with sparkling white trim hugged the rail line. A few wagons waited to be filled with luggage and travelers.

She studied the teeming crowd outside the window. Short, tall, stocky, and lean, the male residents of Lincoln seemed to come in all shapes and sizes. She grinned to herself. Had she expected the men to all look alike?

The train ground to a halt, and she pinned on her hat then took a deep breath. She draped the strap of her reticule over her arm and followed her fellow passengers down the aisle to the exit. Dinah grabbed the handrail and climbed down the steps. She licked her dry lips and longed for a cool glass of water. The merciless sun beat down on her head. She squinted and surveyed the throng.

No one approached or seemed to be searching for her. Tears threatened, and she blinked them away. Her shoulders sagged. Rejected again.

"Miss Reinhardt!"

Her head whipped around to the voice, and her palms slicked with moisture. A broad-shouldered, beefy man hurried toward her, his hand raised above his head. His white shirt was pressed and open at the neck. Worn, but clean, blue jeans covered his legs, and his feet were shod with polished brown boots. A brown Stetson shielded his eyes, but a tentative smile curved his lips. Her pulse raced. Was this handsome man her prospective husband or simply an errand boy sent to do his master's bidding?

He reached her side and removed his hat. "Miss Reinhardt?"

"Ye—" Her voice cracked, and she cleared her throat. "Yes. Are you Mr. Childs?"

"Yes, ma'am." His eyes shuttered. "At your service. Thank you for coming on such short notice."

Dinah's stomach sank. His words said one thing, but his actions another. Was she not the only one harboring a secret?

⸻ ••••●••• ⸻

Nathan forced a smile and held out his arm to the young woman who'd traveled several days to leave everything she knew and start a new life with him. Unsure of what to expect, he was still surprised to discover she was a rather plain woman. Straight, nondescript brown hair fell to her shoulders. Brown eyes studied him from under thin eyebrows in an oval face. Her dark blue suit was rumpled, but that was understandable considering the length of her journey. Her skin was ashen, likely the result of fatigue.

His chest tightened. Looks weren't everything in a person. The Bible called women to be good and kind, fearing the Lord, not charming or beautiful. He'd turned away from Katrina Wainwright because of her spirit. How dare he judge Miss Reinhardt on her appearance.

He cleared his throat. "I don't have a fancy carriage, but my wagon is sturdy enough to carry us home. I'm assuming you brought trunks with you?"

"Two. I'm not sure how to claim them from the baggage car."

"Not to worry. First, I'll get you settled into the vehicle then take care of your belongings."

He led her to his buckboard, looking at the wagon with new eyes. Mrs. Crenshaw had provided very little information about his prospective bride other than to say she was a believer and was leaving a difficult situation, having been attacked on the street. Did she come from wealth? At a minimum, she was a city girl, like Georgianna. Would his prospective bride be able to handle the sparse, sometimes hardscrabble, life on a rural farm?

With unexpected grace, she lifted her skirts and climbed into the wagon. Once seated, she gathered her skirts around herself and gave him a tired, yet triumphant smile. He found himself returning her smile, and his shoulders relaxed.

"I'll return shortly."

She nodded and withdrew a parasol from her bag. Opening it, she held the small umbrella over her head.

His eyes widened. Five minutes together, and she'd already surprised him twice. Would other Eastern women know about the scorching Nebraska sun and be prepared to provide themselves with shade? He pivoted on his heels and hurried to the end of the train where porters had piled trunks, crates, and all manner of luggage on the platform.

Was he making the right decision by agreeing to marry this woman? Would her difficulties follow her to Nebraska? He raked his fingers through his hair and searched among the baggage for her belongings.

Perhaps he should continue raising Florence on his own. He wasn't doing a perfect job, but they made a perfect family, just the two of them. What would a third person, a stranger, do to their relationship? How would Florence feel about Miss Reinhardt? He'd told her she was getting a new mommy, and she'd seemed excited, but did the child understand how her life would change?

Getting to know his prospective wife through a series of letters, like most men did with mail-order brides, would have helped. Instead, he and Miss Reinhardt would have to have become acquainted in the days before the wedding. Would it be enough time to ascertain her true character?

A black trunk and wooden crate bore labels with her name. Another surprise. She hadn't brought enough luggage for an entourage. He beckoned to one of the porters. "A hand, please?"

"Yes, sir." The man hoisted the case on his shoulder with a grunt, then headed toward the wagon.

Nathan bent to lift the crate, and his eyes widened at its weight. What in the world had she brought? He pressed his lips together and hefted the box. Staggering under the burden, he trudged to the buckboard and shoved the crate next to the trunk. He handed the porter a coin then climbed up beside Miss Reinhardt. With a fluid motion, he gathered the reins in his hands and flicked the leather to gently slap the horse's rump. "I'm sure you're exhausted, and we live nearly ten miles away. It's a bit of a drive."

"Thank you. Much appreciated. I'm quite thirsty." Her voice was low and melodic.

He glanced at her through his peripheral vision. She sat ramrod straight under the parasol, her face expressionless. What was she thinking? Did she regret her decision? "How was your journey? Uneventful, I hope."

"Tedious. But I was able to read several books to keep myself entertained."

"Books. That why your crate's so heavy?"

She nodded, and her face brightened. "I love to read."

"As a ranch wife, I'm not sure you'll have a whole lot of time to do that. Too many chores to get done."

Her lips turned down. "Surely, you expect your daughter to learn how to read."

"When she's old enough, but Florence is only three years old. And you'll have a lot to learn about running the house, so best put your education plans on hold for the time being."

"Fine."

He parked the wagon in front of the restaurant and searched his mind for topics. Perhaps a conversation about her hometown would set her at ease. "I lived in Maryland for a while. Pretty state. Lots of hills and trees. What is Baltimore like?"

A wistful smile flitted across her face. "Crowded. The city grew during the war and seems to have expanded even more so since then. But my neighborhood was cozy. Lovely homes with front stoops you could sit on and pass the time."

"Stoops?"

"I guess you call them porches here."

"Ah, yes."

"Anyway, there are also lots of activities to do and sites to visit. Theater, concert performances, and the like."

"Not much of that in Lincoln, I'm afraid. The population has nearly tripled since the war, but people are intent on working, not playing." He swallowed. "Your family make it through the war okay?"

She shrugged. "My brothers were too young and my stepfather too old, but we did lose my cousin at Gettysburg. And friendships, too. Some of those didn't survive."

"I'm sorry about that. Serious differences of opinion tore many families apart. Shame those Southerners couldn't figure out what they were doing was wrong without a fight."

"Have a care, Mr. Childs. Technically, I'm a Southerner, being from below the Mason-Dixon line. Did you know there were plenty of Northerners who owned slaves? Owners hid the fact by calling them apprentices for life. And slavery was not the only issue at stake."

"Yes, ma'am."

He frowned. If possible, her back had gotten even straighter. Was it too late to cable Mrs. Crenshaw and return Miss Reinhardt?

Dinah's Dilemma

Chapter Four

Dinah blinked against the sun's glare, and her gaze swept the room. Momentarily disoriented, she plucked at the colorful quilt on the bed. Events from the previous day flooded her memory, and she sat up. She was in Nebraska. In the bedroom of a man she'd only just met. Wrapping her arms around her middle, she studied her surroundings.

Bright and airy, the room had two windows. Slightly open, they allowed a breeze to flutter the white curtains. A pine dresser sat against one wall, and a pair of nightstands flanked the double bed. In the corner, a framed, full-length mirror captured her wide-eyed expression. Two small watercolors hung above the headboard. Who was the artist? And how wealthy was Mr. Childs that he could afford such a nice house after only a short time on the prairie?

She threw back the covers and set her feet on the floor. Judging from the sun's angle, she'd slept through the morning. Mr. Childs must think her a layabout. Arms overhead, she stretched, her spine crackling with the effort. Next to the mirror, her trunk stood open. She'd considered unpacking last night, but fatigue had overtaken her shortly after dinner, and she'd tumbled into bed after donning her nightgown.

What to do? Unpack or venture into the kitchen?

Her pulse quickened. Then her stomach rumbled, and she grinned. Decision made. She'd see about something to eat then determine her next steps. Quickly changing into a simple skirt and blouse, she brushed the tangles from her hair and pulled the limp strands away from her face with combs Mother had given her as a going-away gift.

Tears pricked the backs of her eyes. Would ever see her family again? She shook her head to clear the morose thoughts, and with a last glance at her reflection, she straightened her spine, opened the door, and walked from the room.

"Good morning. I'm Mrs. Crowell." Hands covered in flour, a middle-aged woman kneaded a lump of dough. "Sleep well, did you?"

Dinah's face heated. "I'm Dinah…uh…Reinhardt. What time is it?"

"Nigh unto ten o'clock. You must be famished." Mrs. Crowell jerked her head toward the cast-iron stove. "I can rustle you up some eggs and toast, if you'd like."

"I can take care of it, if you'll tell me where to find everything."

"This being your first morning and all, you should take it easy. You must still be exhausted from your trip. Besides, the bread needs to sit for a bit before I knead the dough for the second time." A few motions on the pump handle, and water gushed into the sink. She washed and dried her hands then set about making Dinah's meal. "I hope you'll be comfortable here. Nathan and his daughter, Florence, are lovely people."

"When will I get to meet her? She wasn't here when I arrived last night."

"Yes, he thought it best for you to settle in first."

"Or determine if I'm a keeper." Dinah frowned and fiddled with the fringed edge of the woven placemat. "He's been rather aloof, and I'm afraid we disagreed on nearly everything we discussed on the return from the station."

"Nonsense. You're here to stay." Mrs. Crowell scooped the creamy pile of scrambled eggs onto a plate followed by two thick slices of ham then set the dish on the table. "Eat up."

Dinah's mouth watered as she lifted her fork. "This smells divine."

"It's nothing special, but better than train food, I'll wager."

Mouth full, Dinah nodded. While she ate, her gaze ricocheted around the expansive cabin that held a kitchen and fully furnished dining and sitting areas. The oak table had six matching chairs, and the hutch held a full set of china. A blue upholstered sofa and matching chairs nestled around the fireplace, and a well-worn rocking chair sat by one of the windows. Who was this man that he could afford to build and fill a home on a prairie short of wood?

"You'll be wanting a bath, so I'll ask one of the hands to fill the tub. By the time you're ready, I'll need to take care of some chores outside, so you can have privacy."

"I hate to put anyone out."

"Don't be silly. You've traveled far to get here. The least we can do is welcome you with an opportunity to bathe and eat the first decent meal you've had in days. Won't take us long at all." Mrs. Crowell gestured to the bedroom. "Now, you go in there and get what you need. I'll knock when we're ready."

"If you insist…"

"Of course I do." She smiled and patted Dinah's shoulder. "You won't often get the luxury of a day to yourself, so take advantage of it while you can."

Dinah rose and returned to the bedroom where she unpacked her undergarments into the empty dresser then hung her one good dress and her everyday skirts and blouses on the hooks.

A knock sounded. "Your water is ready, miss." A deep voice rumbled from the other side of the door.

"Thank you."

An hour later, she stepped from the tepid water and dried herself before donning a gray calico skirt and white blouse. She slipped on her stockings and shoes then combed her hair and let it hang loose to dry.

Now, to venture outside.

She took a deep breath and opened the door. The porch was wide and welcoming with two rocking chairs and a small table. A slight breeze tickled her cheeks, and the aroma of fresh dirt mingled with the pungent smell of manure. Wheat stalks undulated as far as she could see. The sun shimmered in a cloudless blue sky.

About ten yards from the house, Mrs. Crowell pulled weeds in the vegetable garden. "Did you enjoy yourself, dearie?"

"Yes, thank you for taking such good care of me. I've lollygagged long enough. Will you let me help you?"

"Miss Reinhardt, a word, please." Mr. Childs strode toward the house, a dark scowl on his face.

Dinah's chest tightened. What had she done to anger the man? She hadn't seen him since the prior evening. "Certainly, Mr. Childs. Will you come inside?"

"No. There's work to be done. And I'd appreciate if you'd remember that before you take one of my hands from working in the barn to fill your tub. If you're going to be a successful ranch wife, you need to understand the division of labor. My men are necessary to complete the great number of tasks required each day. You and Mrs. Crowell handle the house and associated chores. Is that clear?"

Her stomach roiled, and breakfast threatened to reappear. He'd apparently jumped to the conclusion that she expected to be waited on and the bath was her idea.

Mrs. Crowell rose. "Nathan—"

"Not now, Mrs. Crowell." He waved her away.

Dinah shook her head at the woman then turned toward Mr. Childs, her spine stiff and unyielding. She would not let him know how much his assumptions and anger hurt. "Yes, sir. Thank you for clarifying my role." She pinned on a sweet smile. "Anything else you'd like to tell me?"

"Uh, no. That will be all for now." His frown faltered. He pivoted and stumbled over the stone border of the flower garden. His feet went out from under him, and he fell against the edge of the porch, then hit the ground. Blood flowed from a large gash on his arm. Moaning, he rolled into a sitting position then attempted to rise.

Dinah dashed down the stairs then dropped to her knees. "Don't move. I can take care of that." No need to tell the man how much first aid she'd performed on her brothers. That would lead to too many questions. She examined the injury, bleeding profusely. "I'll need to stitch your wound. Where are your sewing supplies?"

Before her patient could reply, Mrs. Crowell called from the steps. "I'll get the kit." In moments she returned with a round basket filled with fabric, thread, and a box of pins and needles. From her pocket, she produced a bottle of whiskey. "For his arm. We're not a drinking family."

"Thank you." Dinah uncorked the liquor, aware of Mr. Childs's close scrutiny. Why did he have to be so handsome? "Hold your arm over your head, so the bleeding will stop or at least slow." He complied and her heart thundered in her ears as she poured a measure of alcohol into the laceration.

He hissed and closed his eyes.

"I'm sorry, but the whiskey should prevent infection."

Teeth gritted, he nodded.

She cleaned and stitched the wound, brow furrowed in concentration. Her first morning was definitely not going as anticipated. Finished, she snipped the end of the thread and inspected her work. Not perfect, and he'd probably have a scar, but he should heal. She wrapped a piece of fabric around the arm to cover the injury. "You might want to have the doctor look at that."

His eyes opened, and he looked at the cotton floral bandage. "I'm not sure it goes with my outfit."

Packing the supplies, she giggled, then rose and gripped the basket to herself. "Perhaps you should have had one of your ranch hands do the job. Now, don't you have work to do?"

He grunted as he climbed to his feet. Flushed, he ducked his head. "Listen, Miss Reinhardt, I uh…may have overreacted earlier. I don't know how to do this. My daughter is in desperate need of a mother, and Mrs. Crenshaw seemed to provide a solution, but now that you're here…"

Dinah squinted and cocked her head. "You're regretting your decision. Say no more, Mr. Childs. I will stay and be a mother to your daughter, should you wish, but I have no foolish notions that you could ever possibly love me. I'll be inside when you've made your decision. Lunch will be ready in an hour." She pulled her skirts close and marched into the house, closing the door with a muted thud. Leaning against the smooth wood, she bowed her head, lips trembling.

Father, what will I do if he rejects me? I don't want to go home even though he will never love me as a wife. I haven't met his daughter, but I'd like to stay and raise her to love You. Is that why You arranged for me to come to Nebraska? To bring Your love to this family? If so, help me, because right now I don't feel up to the task.

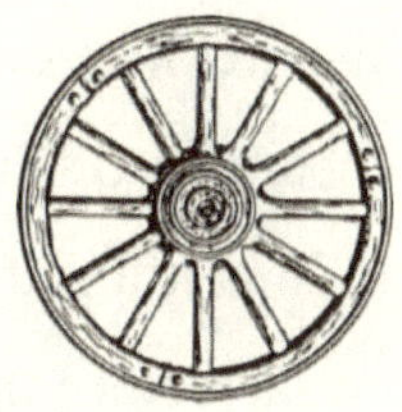

Chapter Five

Perspiration adhered Nathan's shirt to his back as he nailed the last board into place in the barn. Several planks between the stalls were rotted and should have been replaced long before now, but planting took precedence followed by myriad other tasks of importance. His farmhands worked hard, but he still couldn't afford as many as were required to maintain a property of this size.

Cinnamon, his favorite bay horse, whinnied from across the barn. He smiled and glanced at the majestic animal. "Making too much noise, am I? Been a while since we've been able to go for a ride to nowhere. Maybe later."

The horse nickered and bobbed his head as if he understood.

Nathan shook his head. He'd always talked with his animals, but if Miss Reinhardt, Dinah, caught him, she might think him off his rocker. They'd agreed to call each other by their given names, and he liked the way hers felt when he used it. "Ugh. Come on, Childs, you've got work to do. Quit daydreaming." Now, he was talking to himself. She'd really think he was cuckoo.

He gathered his tools, his three-day-old wound tender but not painful, and moved to the buckboard. Had Dinah learned to stitch angry gashes during the war? She hadn't mentioned serving as a nurse, but they'd avoided discussing the conflict since the ride from the station when he'd offended her.

Mrs. Crowell had dropped more than a few strong hints that Dinah might appreciate a padded seat on the vehicle, a luxury he'd never considered. No upholsterer, he'd filled some feed sacks with straw. He tossed them into the wagon and climbed on board. Bent over the seat with nails held between his lips, he tacked the puffy bags to the seat plank.

Cocking his head, he studied his attempt. He pushed down on the pads. Enough cushion, but the straw prickled his palm through the burlap. That wouldn't do. What to use? He swung his head searching for something, anything, that might soften the seat. Draped over a sawhorse was the piece of rawhide he'd tanned last fall. Unsure what he wanted to do with the supple leather, he'd left it in the barn until he could decide.

The hide would fetch a good price in town, or he could use it for something much more practical, but padding the wagon was the unselfish thing to do. He jumped down from the buckboard and strode across the barn. Grabbing the skin, he inhaled the earthy, slightly sweet smell of the leather. Supple, yet strong, the piece should hold up against wear and tear, yet provide a soft alternative to the feed sacks. With quick motions, he covered the burlap pads then stepped back to admire the finished project.

He looked forward to seeing Dinah's pleased expression at the seat. He liked when she smiled. And he enjoyed watching her interact with Florence, who smiled more since Dinah's arrival than she had in the previous year. Had he dragged down his daughter's moods with his sadness?

His heart tugged, and he rubbed the back of his neck. Would he ever stop missing his sweet wife? The move to Nebraska was supposed to be a new start, but he'd apparently packed his grief along with the household goods. Georgianna had never lived in the lush plains, but he saw her everywhere he looked.

With a deep breath, he jumped from the wagon. He grabbed his tools and returned them to the box where they were stored. Parched, he licked his dry lips then clapped his Stetson over his sweaty hair and headed to the house. A tall glass of water was in order.

At the sight of Florence and Dinah kneeling side by side in a freshly dug garden in front of the porch, he froze. Brow furrowed in concentration, his daughter plunked some sort of flower into the ground, then scooped soil in the hole and pressed the dirt firmly around the plant. "Did I do good, Miss Dinah?"

Dinah beamed. "You did *well*, Florence. Isn't this pretty?"

"I like it."

Nathan crossed his arms and continued to watch the interchange, his heart full at the sight of his happy daughter.

"What is your favorite color, Florence?"

The three-year-old cocked her head and tapped her chin as if she were determining the fate of the universe. "Red…no…pink. I have two favorites. Is that okay?"

"Of course it is." Dinah gently touched the petals of the flower they'd planted. "All of God's creation is beautiful. It's difficult to pick just one. Isn't it wonderful that He gave us so many different plants and trees and animals? He could have created only a few, or even one or two, and we wouldn't have known any better. But He loves us so much, He wanted us to have pretty things to look at."

"God is good, isn't He, Miss Dinah."

She touched the tip of Florence's nose. "That He is, honey."

"What color do you like best?"

"Yellow, because it reminds me of the sun, and I especially love daisies because they have a bright yellow center."

"I don't know daisies." Florence scrunched up her face. "Do we have daisies?"

"I didn't see any when we collected the wildflowers, but perhaps one of the ladies at church has some to share. Do daisies grow in Nebraska?"

Florence shrugged. "You should ask Daddy. He'll know. He knows everything."

"Does he? We'll ask him at dinner tonight."

Nathan's chest puffed out. His daughter thought he knew everything. He grinned. Wait until she was a teenager. That would change. But for now, he'd take her adulation.

He took off his hat and fanned himself, but the act only served to push the hot air around his face. Gripping the brim, he leaned against the fence that separated the barn and house. His eyebrows shot up as Dinah crouched and tugged at a fair-sized rock at the edge of the garden. Did she think she could move the stone?

When the boulder didn't budge, she picked up a trowel and scooped away the surrounding dirt then pushed the rock back and forth. Should he help her, or would she see his assistance as interference?

Dinah swiped at her forehead, and a muddy smudge darkened her skin. With renewed vigor, she attacked the ground, exposing the sides of the boulder. "Okay, stand back, honey. I'm going to pull out the rock." Standing, she bent over the stone and pulled. Her hands slipped, and she fell back and landed on her backside.

"Miss Reinhardt." Nathan rushed forward. "Dinah. Are you all right?"

She turned, her face pink. Exertion or embarrassment?

He grabbed her hand, and tingles convulsed his fingers. Wide eyed, he wrapped his arm around her shoulders. "Don't move. You could be hurt."

She giggled. "Only my pride, Mr. Childs…er…Nathan. I'm fine." Her cheeks deepened to a bright red, and she waved him away. "I may have some bruises to show for my foolishness." She poked at the rock. "This must be like an iceberg, with only a small percentage of the actual density aboveground."

"I can take care of that for you." He smiled. "You need only to ask."

"No, you have your tasks, and I have mine. Besides, a little strenuous exercise is good for us."

"Always the teacher, eh, Dinah? I heard you with Florence telling her about God's creation. Thank you for opening her eyes to Him. I haven't talked about God since…well…" He cleared his throat. "Since her mother passed."

"But He can help you with your grief."

"A great theory, Dinah, but I haven't found that to be so in reality." He shrugged. "How could God let an innocent woman die?" He stood and shoved his hands into his pockets. "I couldn't save her from the fire, but neither did He."

Dinah climbed to her feet. "Fire?"

"During one of my assignments with Pinkerton. Local officials expected trouble during an election, so they hired several of us agents. There were a few ugly incidents with one of the gangs, but we were able to squelch any serious situations. Several of the members were arrested, but quite a few of them managed to escape. My home, and those of three of the other agents burned to the ground." His breathing hitched. "My wife was home alone, and she was either asleep or overcome by smoke. She never made it out of the house. Fortunately, Florence was visiting my folks. Investigations later proved the fires were arson."

"Oh, Nathan." She touched his arm, and the warmth of her fingers created a jolt that shot to his elbow. "I'm so sorry. Where did this happen?"

"Maryland, outside of Baltimore." He cocked his head. "Living there, you must have heard about the fires."

She paled and shook her head. "My mother tried to shelter me from disturbing news, especially during the war."

"This was almost three years ago, shortly after Florence was born."

Sorrow and some other emotion he couldn't read flitted across her face. Regret? Anger? Guilt? Odd reactions, to be sure. His investigative senses bristled. Was she hiding something? Was she no different than Katrina? Another woman whose life was comprised of lies? Mrs. Crenshaw may have done a background check, but it was time to get Alfred involved. No doubt the sheriff had deeper contacts than the wealthy widow. No wedding would take place until he was sure Dinah posed to no threat to Florence.

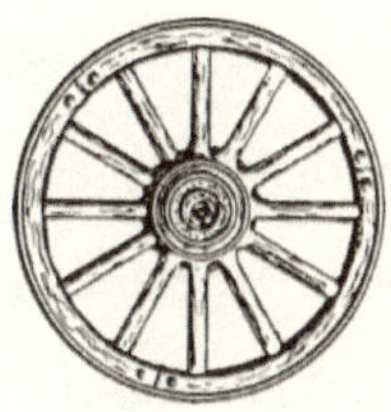

Chapter Six

With her fork, Dinah drew lines in her mashed potatoes. Rich brown gravy flowed from the creamy mixture and pooled under her peas. Her stomach flip-flopped. For the first time since her arrival, she'd helped prepare dinner, and thus far, Nathan, as he'd ask her to call him, saying formalities didn't belong on the prairie, hadn't said one word about the meal. Had she failed? Did he not enjoy the food? Or did he simply not care one whit?

Florence must have felt the tension because after her initial chattering, she'd fallen silent, poking bite after bite into her mouth. In the five days since Dinah's arrival, the child had latched on to her with surprising warmth. After two days, she'd started the habit of crawling into her lap after the dinner chores were completed and listen while Dinah read from *Hans Brinker, or The Silver Skates* or *Elsie Dinsmore*. Her supply of children's books was limited, but Florence didn't seem to mind the repetition.

She glanced at the watch on her bodice and sighed. What time was it in Baltimore? Were her parents eating dinner together, feeling her absence. Where were her brothers? Hunkered down trying to avoid capture for some misdeed? Her heart tugged. As much as she missed her family, she'd begun to relax while in Nebraska, no longer having to worry about finances or whether the police would show up at the door and ask probing questions.

"Eat your peas, sweetie. Don't play with them." Nathan smiled at Florence.

"But I don't like them, Daddy." Florence frowned.

Dinah stifled a snicker at the child's matter-of-fact voice as if her explanation would convince her father that she didn't need to consume the offending vegetable. She patted Florence's arm and wrinkled her nose. "I don't care for them either, but they're good for us. Sometimes we have to do things we don't want to."

Florence gaped at her then nodded and scooped a forkful of peas into her mouth. She chewed quickly then swallowed with a grimace. Grabbing her cup, she took a swig of milk.

"Good girl." Nathan winked at his daughter. "Thank you," he mouthed to Dinah then dropped his gaze.

Her face warmed. Would their awkwardness ever disappear? Or did she only imagine the clumsiness of their interactions? She cleared her throat. "Did you get everything done today you desired?"

He laid down his fork and nodded. "Yes, thank you for asking. We finished the fence repairs in one section and got the calves branded, among other tasks. How about you? Was your day productive?"

"Yes, Mrs. Crowell and I did laundry, and I was able to mend your shirts. Plus, I had time to bake a cake."

"Yay, cake!" Florence clapped her hands. "I love cake."

Dinah lifted one eyebrow. "But there won't be any dessert until we've finished *all* our food."

Florence sagged. "Peas, too?"

"Peas, too." Dinah stroked the child's silky hair. "I promise you, the cake will be a worthy reward, so eat up."

"You finish yours, Mama Dinah."

Nathan's head whipped up, his eyes glittering. "When did she start calling you that?"

"Uh, this morning. I'm sorry, should I not allow her to use the term?"

He studied her for a long moment, and she squirmed under his scrutiny.

"No, that's fine. I'm surprised. That's all."

"No less than you." Dinah wiped her lips with her napkin, pushed to her feet, spine stiff, and went to the pie safe. She opened the door and pulled out the twelve-layer, chocolate-frosted cake then set the plate in the center of the table. "This is called a Smith Island cake from the small islands in the Chesapeake Bay. It is said that the watermen's wives would send the cakes with their husbands on the autumn oyster harvest to remind them of the families they'd left behind." She shrugged. "Although I can't imagine traveling on a boat and trying to keep this from pitching into the water."

"Your tale and your cake are impressive." Nathan rose, collected the dirty dishes, and took them to the sink. "Must have required a lot of work. I appreciate the efforts you're making. I know it hasn't been easy." He handed her three small plates.

Her pulse raced. A compliment. And recognition of her attempts to fit in. She cut the cake and placed a generous slice on his plate and smaller ones for her and Florence. "This is my mother's recipe. I hope you like it." She might never measure up to his late wife, but she had value, and she loved his little girl. Surely, that counted for something. There had to be ways to make him happy and to accept her. She wouldn't rest until she'd learned everything she could about the dead woman. Only then would she know whether she had a chance of success.

⸻ ••◦◉◦•• ⸻

Nathan forked a piece of the cake into his mouth. Flavors exploded on his tongue. When he'd first seen the decadent-looking treat, he'd almost blurted out a reprimand for using a large percentage of their baking supplies. He'd manage to keep his thoughts to himself, but at some point he'd have to discuss the need to ration their goods. Frugality was crucial on the prairie. She'd need to learn to conserve, earlier rather than later. Why had Mrs. Crowell not said anything to her?

He made quick work of the cake and sat back. "Delicious." Her face pinked. Was she not used to receiving praise? It was good she could cook. What other skills did she possess? She'd repaired his shirts, but he hadn't seen them yet to assess her abilities. Georgianna had been an excellent seamstress, her stitches tiny and regular. Her fancy work was intricate and beautiful. She also had been an accomplished cook, making meals fit for a king even during the early years of their marriage.

Would he never stop missing her? Seeing her face in his mind's eye? Looking for her in every corner of his world, no matter where he lived? His heart dropped. Would he have married her if he knew the pain in store for him with her death? Even if he wanted to, opening his heart to Dinah was not wise. Love only led to sorrow, and she could never compare to his wife.

Meal complete, Dinah rose and began to clear the table. "Would you watch Florence while I do the dishes?"

"How about if I wash, and you read to both of us?" Nathan blinked. Where had that come from? He never performed household chores.

A smile bloomed on her face. "That would be lovely. Thank you."

He returned her smile, his breath catching. Her porcelain skin glowed in the flickering candlelight, her eyes sparkling. Her hair shimmered and fell in soft-looking tresses around her face. Why had he thought her unattractive? What had changed? It was his turn to duck and turn away. Since when was he shy with women? He blew out a breath and went to the sink, filling the basin with water.

Still smiling, Dinah disappeared into her bedroom, then returned moments later carrying Jules Verne's *Journey to the Center of the Earth*. She settled into the rocking chair, and as anticipated, Florence climbed into her lap, thumb stuck between her lips. She nestled against Dinah's chest, her eyes closed. "I'm not sure how much she'll understand, but I thought the Dinsmore family could use a break."

His eyes widened at the scene of his daughter nestled into Dinah's embrace, and he turned back to the sink, determined to ignore the various emotions that battled for supremacy. "As can we." He spoke over his shoulder.

"Nebraska looks nothing like Maryland, but the landscape is gorgeous. When the wheat sways in the breeze, the motion reminds me of the waves on the bay. Wrong color, of course, but still reminiscent of the water." Sadness colored her voice. "Had you visited here before when you decided to move?"

"I'd been to the state once for an assignment with Pinkerton. It was still a territory when I came, but I fell in love with the rugged, stark plains and knew I'd end up here. I chose Lincoln because of my deep appreciation for the president." His face warmed as he rinsed the plates and laid them on a towel to dry. "Sounds foolish when I say that out loud."

"I admired him, too. He was a great man who died too early." She laid the book on the table at her elbow. "I saw him once. He stopped in

Baltimore during his campaign. Mother and Father didn't think it proper for me to go, but I slipped out of the house to hear him speak. I'm glad I did. He was so articulate. Made me reconsider many of my opinions."

He chuckled at the thought of her scuttling out the door and hiding among the crowds along the railroad tracks. He'd been there, hired by Pinkerton himself to thwart a supposed assassination attempt. What would he have thought of her if he'd seen her?

"Would you like to go into town tomorrow? I'm sure you could use a break from the isolation on the ranch."

She beamed, then her smile faltered. "Are you sure you have time for a trip? I don't want to impede your work."

"I'm not too busy, and I'd be honored to accompany you."

"Thank you." She giggled, the sound low and melodic.

He realized he was grinning like a schoolboy who had won first prize in the calf-roping contest. What had he done? One minute he vowed to remain aloof, the next he had plans to spend the day with her. Why did life have to be so complicated?

Dinah's Dilemma

Chapter Seven

Despite the overcast skies and her parasol, perspiration trickled down Dinah's back as the wagon bounced over the rutted road on the way into Lincoln. The padded seat Nathan had installed was a blessing, and he'd reddened when she thanked him profusely for his thoughtfulness. He'd ducked and stammered like a schoolboy, a side of him she'd not seen in the days since her arrival.

Dust clouds puffed at her face, kicked up by the horse's steady plodding. She waved her hand in a futile effort to dispel the choking powdery substance.

Nathan glanced over then pulled a clean handkerchief from his pocket. "I should have thought about the dust. Wrap this around your nose and mouth. Some rain would do us good for a number of reasons."

She took the hanky, her fingers brushing his hand. Tingles shot up her arm. Did he feel that? She folded the fabric into a triangle then tied two corners into a knot behind her head. Ah, sweet relief. "We won't be mistaken for cattle rustlers or bank robbers, will we?"

He grinned, his eyes crinkling at the corners. "I doubt it, especially with your Sunday-go-to-meeting outfit, complete with lace umbrella. Should I have dressed up?"

A giggle escaped, and her face heated, having nothing to do with the weather. "No. It's just…well, I enjoy wearing pretty dresses and won't have too much opportunity on the farm. Not practical, but I hope you don't mind."

"Not at all. You look lovely. But the gals in town might be jealous of how nice you look. Don't take it personally."

The wagon hit a deep hole, jerking the contraption to the side and nearly pitching her over the side. She grabbed Nathan's arm, his skin warm to her touch even through his shirt sleeve. She pulled back as if scalded, a nervous laugh bursting from her lips. "Sorry. Perhaps you should have added some sort of strap to keep me on board."

He threw back his head and laughed. "Guess you're used to those fancy carriages with sides and doors. Should I keep a grip on you?"

Her heart skipped at his carefree expression. She hadn't seen it often, usually only when he was with Florence. Otherwise, he wore a shroud of grief that set his face into harsh lines. Good looking in mourning, he was devastatingly handsome in joy. Cobalt-blue eyes set wide in his tanned face, hovered over an aquiline nose and firm chin. Short and neatly trimmed, his beard accented his square jaw. A bear of a man, he had a broad chest and wide shoulders.

"Dinah? Where did you go?"

"Oh…uh…" She forced a smile. Could her face get any hotter? "Considering your offer."

With a chuckle, he shook his head. Holding the reins loosely in his calloused hands, he leaned his elbows on his knees.

She licked her dry lips. Why did she get so tongue tied around Nathan? She'd held court with important men in Baltimore's drawing rooms. "Can you tell me about your work with the Pinkertons? Were you ever afraid? The work must be dangerous."

"Dangerous, yes, but rewarding." A shadow passed over his face. "Although I wasn't able to save Lincoln from assassination."

"Were you at the theater?"

"No." He shook his head. "I'd been assigned to one of the senators that night because one of the other agents took sick. But as if I knew something was going to happen, I was restless, fitful. I had trouble concentrating. Then I heard about the president. A tragedy."

"Yes. I feel badly for Mrs. Lincoln. She's suffered so many losses."

"Indeed, and there is concern about Tad. I've heard he's been ill."

"Oh no." Dinah brushed an errant strand of hair from her face. "Do you miss the excitement? Is life at the farm tedious in comparison?"

"Not in the least. I like being my own boss, and there's great satisfaction in making the property yield produce and sustain cattle. I needed a change, and so did Florence. She'd already lost one parent." His voice broke, and he cleared his throat. "She shouldn't have to worry about losing a second one."

"I didn't mean to make you sad."

He shrugged. "You didn't. The feeling is constant." He hunched into himself, his mouth set in a slash.

She fell silent as the wagon creaked and groaned on its journey. Her chest tightened. Had she made the right decision coming West to make a home with a grieving widower? She didn't have to fear for her life or reputation out here, but the aura of gloom clung to the farm like a cloak, and even though Nathan's wife was gone, she was certainly never forgotten, impacting every moment of every day.

Meet him where he is, My child, and show him love and acceptance. He needs time to heal.

Dinah blinked. She'd never received such a strong command before. A gentle nudge or perhaps a feeling, but never words in her head. *Okay, Lord. I'll do as You ask, but how long will it take? His wife has already been gone for three years.* Guilt pricked her heart, and she sighed. Who was she to bargain with God? He'd given her a task, and like the prophet Jeremiah, she'd do as He asked. Hopefully, it wouldn't take forty years. *Please protect my heart.* She shifted on the seat, her shoulder bumping Nathan's solid form. "Ah…so…did you want to tell me more about the Pinkertons? Did you have any particularly challenging cases?"

He glanced at her, his eyes clouded and distant.

Should she start talking to fill the silence? Would chattering only serve to irritate him?

"Yes, especially those I worked undercover. Those cases are also the most dangerous. Twice, I infiltrated a gang, and they would have killed me without a second thought if they'd discovered my identity."

A chill swept over her. Had he met her brothers? Did he know them? Did he know her relationship to them but acted like he didn't as a ploy to get her to open up about them? "How frightening. Which gangs?"

"I can't say. Allen Pinkerton swears his agents to secrecy, and even though I'm no longer in his employ, the agreement holds."

"I understand. You must be very brave."

Nathan lifted one shoulder. "No more so than other men. Pinkerton trained us extensively, so I always felt prepared to go into the situation."

Dinah wiped a damp palm on her skirt. Was she prepared for the situation? Had she gone from the frying pan into the fire? What if Nathan found out about her brothers? Would he paint her with the same brush like other people did…assuming she'd perpetrated crimes alongside Herbert and Jerome? *Oh Lord, are You sure I'm supposed to stay and help Nathan?*

• • • ● • • •

Nathan cast a sidelong glance at Dinah. Her expression was guarded. Since leaving the homestead, she'd alternately been curious and cautious. Perhaps living in Baltimore had given her an up-close view of the gangs. Had she somehow been exposed to the seamy side of the city with its violence and deceitful dealings? Had she suffered at their hands? Did she know something she wasn't telling?

He nibbled on his lower lip. If he asked, would she tell him?

The wagon lurched, and her hip bumped his leg. His eyes widened, and he swallowed, forcing himself to continue their conversation. "The other thing Pinkerton does for his agents is to provide backup. I was never far from help."

"You said you were undercover. Were you a spy during the war?" Her voice was hard.

"No." Did she object to the thought of using subterfuge to achieve victory? "I was in the army until sixty-three then moved to guarding the president and other people of importance. Rumors of assassination plots abounded, so the necessity arose to surround Lincoln with armed escorts." He winked at her. "Were you a spy?"

A quick intake of breath, then she wrinkled her nose. "I was fifteen when the war started. Hardly in a position to perform clandestine activities."

"Not necessarily. But you've mentioned your parents protected you from the news. Did they keep you under close watch as well?"

"Yes. Another reason my efforts would have been thwarted."

"Too bad. I think you'd have done well. You've come West, so you're willing to take risks. You're trying a lifestyle you've never been exposed to which indicates you're willing to go into the unknown. Two traits Mr. Pinkerton holds in high regard."

She reddened and ducked her head. Something told him she rarely received compliments. What kind of parents did she have? He blew out a loud breath. "The war changed everything, didn't it? I'm not sure I would have ended up with the agency if it wasn't for my service in the military. What would you be doing if you weren't riding in a buckboard in Nebraska?"

Uncertainty flickered in her eyes, then she stiffened. "I wanted to be a teacher, but my most recent application was rejected. One of the reasons I took Mrs. Crenshaw's offer to be one of her mail-order brides. I didn't see a future in Maryland. A fresh start in another state seemed providential."

"You'd make a wonderful teacher. I see you with Florence, making the most mundane chores into an adventure or lesson. She's blossomed under your tutelage."

"She's a delightful child and creates adventure on her own." Dinah smiled. "You must have had your hands full with her. She's fearless."

Memories of Florence approaching the animal pens at the fair shot through Nathan's mind. "I considered putting her in a harness and reins after she started walking. She wandered off on a regular basis, and I had a dickens of a time keeping up with her."

Dinah laughed and clapped her hands, her face lighting up. "A clever idea. I bet lots of parents would purchase a child's tackle set. You may be onto something."

His chest swelled at her admiration. "Perhaps if this farm thing doesn't work out, I could try my hand at making and selling baby harnesses." The wagon rounded the bend and entered the burgeoning town. Horses whinnied, people shouted and laughed, and carriages rattled as they bounced down the main thoroughfare.

"I'll drop you off at the mercantile and meet you there. I need to stop in the sheriff's office and see Alfred. Take all the time you need."

Her face paled, and an expression akin to fear flashed in her eyes. What in her background would give rise to anxiety at the mention of the law? Was it too early to follow up with his friend to see if he'd turned up anything about his prospective bride?

Chapter Eight

Nathan set the brake on the wagon and jumped to the ground. He walked to Dinah's side of the vehicle and helped her climb down. Warmth from her hand spread up his arm, yet goose bumps rose on his skin. He stifled a shiver as she smiled her thanks and ascended the steps into the general store, her expression still shuttered. The bell jangled when she opened the door.

He lifted his Stetson and raked his fingers through his hair. Courting Georgianna hadn't been nearly this challenging. Sweet and docile, she'd never contradicted him or his opinion, instead, choosing to follow his lead, no questions asked. There had also been no secrets between them. Dinah, on the other hand, seemed a bundle of secrecy, and she spoke her mind, not hesitating to disagree. She wasn't argumentative, but neither was she pliant.

His daughter adored her. Every day, the child seemed to fall more in love with his prospective bride. He'd grown accustomed to Florence's usage of the phrase Mama Dinah. He enjoyed watching the two of them interact. Curious before Dinah had come, she now sought to explore everything in her little world. She'd even asked for help learning to read. He smiled. Were all fathers as enamored with their little girls as him?

Waiting for horses and carriages to pass, he surveyed the pedestrians. Town was busy this morning. Women with baskets looped over their arms darted in and out of the shops, children tagging behind. Men gathered, presumably discussing crops, animals, and the weather, always a popular topic, especially during the growing season. Too early to serve their firewater, the saloons were dark and quiet.

Plunking his hat on his head, he stepped off the wooden walkway and crossed the dirt street, dust clouds rising under his boots. Rain would be a blessing. Too many days since any moisture had fallen from the sky.

He headed into the sheriff's office, his eyes adjusting to the dim lighting. Alfred leaned back in the chair, his feet propped on the desk, and his nose buried in the newspaper. He folded the broadsheet and cocked his head. "A little unusual for you to be in town when you could be taking advantage of a beautiful day to get things done around the farm."

"Is that a question?" Nathan dropped into a rickety wooden chair that creaked in protest. He crossed his legs and balanced his hat on his knee.

"Nah, just an observation." Alfred winked. "Although if you have something to tell me, I'm all ears."

"I'm here to see if you have anything to tell me. You sent for information about Dinah, right? Have you heard from your sources?"

"Exactly how much do you think I can find out in less than a week?"

Nathan shrugged. "Didn't you use the telegraph system? Not like you had to use the Pony Express."

"True, but we gotta give the guys on the other end time to do their job. Relax." The sheriff narrowed his eyes. "Something happen that's giving you pause?"

"Yes. No."

Alfred chuckled. "Well, which is it?"

"I'm not sure." Nathan blew out a deep breath. "Dinah seems nice enough, and I can't put my finger on it, but my gut tells me she's hiding something."

"Maybe she's simply overwhelmed with moving out here and the idea of marrying you. That would cause any woman to act a little skittish."

"Funny. I'm serious. A couple of times we've talked, and she gets a look on her face, almost like she's guilty."

"What were you discussing at the time?" Alfred laced his fingers and put them behind his head. "Is it one particular topic that seems to…I don't know…upset her?"

"The first time we were talking about the war—"

"That disturbs everyone."

"Yeah, but her response seemed personal. Anyway, she also seems agitated about my time as a Pinkerton agent. Both times we've talked she was jumpy." Nathan rubbed his forehead. "I don't know. Maybe I'm imagining things. Maybe I've seen too many bad guys which makes me look at everyone with suspicion."

"I get like that sometimes. Olivia has to remind me that not everyone is a thief or a crook."

"Hazard of the job, I suppose."

"Give our guys some more time to respond. Another week, at least. Mrs. Crenshaw wouldn't have sent Dinah if she didn't think the girl was okay. Propose already. You know that widow-woman is fairly close to the good Lord himself, so you should be in the clear."

Nathan shoved himself to his feet. "Thanks for taking care of this…and for being the voice of reason. I'm not sure I'm ready to propose, but I'll consider your suggestion."

"You've done the same for me." Alfred lifted the newspaper. "I'll be praying for you, friend."

"Should be doing more of that myself." With a half-hearted wave, Nathan let himself out of the office.

The sky had cleared while he was inside, and the sun beat down on the bustling activity. Donning his hat against the glare, he trotted across the street and entered the mercantile.

In the far corner, Dinah stood at the fabric counter with Amanda Garlinger, the shop owner's wife. Thin and angular, Mrs. Garlinger was the exact opposite of her husband, William, who was as wide as he was tall. They adored each other, and had plenty of warmth to share, but were unable to have children. Instead, they poured their love into their community, and it appeared the woman was already drawing Dinah under her wing.

They chatted as if old friends, although this was only Dinah's second visit to the store. Her face wreathed in smiles, she nodded as Mrs. Garlinger talked. Dinah giggled then responded, her hands waving as if she were conducting music. The more she spoke, the faster her hands moved. Why hadn't he noticed her habit of talking with her hands?

He grinned, and the tension in his shoulders melted away. Alfred was right. Mrs. Crenshaw would not have recommended Dinah as a bride if she didn't believe her trustworthy. His time as an agent made him suspicious of everyone. He'd come to Nebraska for a fresh start. It was time he embraced the change.

Stuffing his hands into his pockets, he approached the women. "Good morning, ladies."

Dinah's head whipped around, and she smiled, her eyes lighting up.

Mrs. Garlinger pecked him on the cheek. "Nathan, how wonderful to see you. Thank you for bringing your friend to see us. She's absolutely lovely."

Cheeks pink, Dinah lowered her gaze.

"She is, isn't she?" He fingered a bolt of blue calico fabric. "I hope this is one of your selections, Dinah. You look nice in blue."

Her smile faltered. "I hadn't planned to pick up any dressmaking material."

"Plans change. Mrs. Garlinger, please package however much she needs of this to make an outfit." He turned to Dinah. "Select two other colors as well. Might make you feel better to have some new clothes."

"You're very generous." She sounded breathless, yet she seemed happy.

He studied her face. Was she ill? "And when you're done shopping, let's grab a bite to eat at the restaurant before heading home."

"That would be wonderful. I'm nearly finished here."

"No hurry. I need a few things for the farm, too." He tipped his hat at the ladies and wandered the shelves, selecting the items, and carrying them to the checkout counter.

Fifteen minutes later, their goods were in the back of the wagon, and they were seated in the restaurant awaiting their order. Early for lunch, only one other couple filled a table. Nathan watched as Dinah gazed around the room, drinking in her surroundings.

A stray hair had pulled from her bun, and his fingers itched to tuck the silky-looking strand behind her ear. Better yet, what would it be like to pull down her tightly wound bun? His eyes widened, and he shook his head to clear the thought. "The restaurant must not be as posh as you're used to. Baltimore has some fantastic places to eat."

She turned toward him. "My family is not as well-to-do as you assume, Nathan. The last time I visited one of the so-called posh places was before the war. This is very nice. Clean, too. Thank you for bringing me into town. Do you eat here often when you're picking up supplies?"

"No. Mrs. Crowell usually packs sandwiches that I consume on the road."

"We could have eaten in the wagon if you're in a hurry to get back." She frowned. "I didn't think about the fact that your absence means some chores aren't getting done."

He squeezed her hand. "There is nothing that can't wait until tomorrow, and I made the decision to come to Lincoln. You didn't push me into the trip, so there's no need to apologize."

The waitress appeared with two plates of steaming food and set them on the table. "Anything else, Mr. Childs?"

"No, thank you, Iris. Tell your mom she's outdone herself as usual. Lunch smells delicious."

She nodded and made her way to the other couple's table.

Nathan said grace, and they dug into their meal.

"Sweet girl." Dinah scooped gravy-covered mashed potatoes onto her fork and popped them into her mouth. Her eyes closed for a moment, and she moaned. "These are divine."

He chuckled. "Matilda Spielman is the best cook west of the Mississippi. Maybe east, too. Mrs. Crowell doesn't like for me to mention my meals here. I think she gets jealous."

"Then I won't say anything about our visit." Dinah giggled. "I don't want to hurt her feelings."

"Good girl." He grinned. "This will be our little secret."

Her eyes flashed in the flickering oil lamp. "Don't saddle me with too many of them."

"Have trouble keeping confidences, do you?" He laughed.

She cocked her head. "Reminiscent of having to watch what I said during the war, wondering who was on which side of the conflict, trying not to offend or inadvertently give away information. Not that I had any, but Mother said a person couldn't be too careful. Recently, we've had to keep a lid on Father's gambling problems. Tiresome, really."

"I'm sorry to dredge up bad memories."

"Don't be. Now that I'm here, they're starting to fade. The beauty of the land. No one looking down their nose at me or whispering behind their hands. Florence. Dear Florence. She's the best part of being here."

"Not me?" Putting on an exaggerated look of shock, he pressed one hand against his chest and put the other on his forehead. "I'm deeply wounded, Miss Reinhardt."

Her jaw dropped, then seconds later she clapped her hands and laughed. "You had me going, *Mister* Childs." She swatted his arm and continued to giggle. "Perhaps a career on the stage should be your next venture."

He chuckled and leaned on the table. "Got you good, didn't I?"

Dinah wiggled her eyebrows. "And I will get you back."

"I look forward to it." His pulse quickened. Dinah was a good and kind woman, and she made him laugh, look at things with fresh eyes. No, she wasn't Georgianna, but that didn't seem to matter anymore. Should he take Alfred's advice and propose?

Chapter Nine

The sun dipped toward the horizon, creating long shadows as the wagon bumped its way back to the farm. Parasol no longer necessary, Dinah sat with hands laced in her lap. A comfortable silence hung between her and Nathan. Reins held loosely in his fingers, he seemed to be letting the horse determine their pace, which was fine with her. There would be time enough for busyness and chores once they reached the homestead.

She glanced at Nathan and smiled. The day had started with uncertainty and was ending with confidence. Confidence that she could succeed as a farmer's wife and raise his daughter, and perhaps their own children if so blessed. He might not ever love her, but he was making an effort to treat her with respect and decency, and she would guard her heart to prevent the hurt of rejection. A God-fearing man who provided for his family was more than many women had, so she'd take what she was given and be grateful.

Warm breezes brushed her face, and she raised one hand to her cheek. With few trees on the plains, the wind was a constant. Good for drying the laundry, bad for a girl's skin. Perhaps it was time to swap her Baltimore hats for a prairie bonnet. She frowned. One more adjustment to her ever-changing life. A small transition, but disconcerting nonetheless. Would her days eventually settle into a sense of normalcy? Or will she always feel off kilter?

"Penny for your thoughts." Nathan's voice rumbled in his chest. "You haven't said much since we left town. Are you all right?"

"Yes. Just lost in thought. Nebraska is so different from Maryland, yet beautiful in its own way. The vast fields of corn and wheat are overwhelming, and I had nothing to do with them this season, but in some strange way there's a great sense of satisfaction looking at them. I've only had a taste of the amount of work to produce the crops, but the number of chores must be exhausting." She nudged his shoulder. "I'm impressed."

He chuckled, his face reddening under his tan. "I had help."

"I know, but you're in charge of everything. Aren't you afraid of the farm failing?"

"Not as much as I used to be. Even though the community is far flung, the families are close knit, and we watch out for each other, providing for needs as they arise. My home is a perfect example. Most of these folks live in sod homes. I didn't want that for Florence, so I paid an extraordinary amount of money to have supplies shipped here. Rather than be jealous or judgmental about the extravagance, my neighbors and several people from town came together and helped me build the house. Winters can be harsh, and we check in with each other periodically."

Dinah widened her eyes. "Quite different from Baltimore where those who fall on hard times are ridiculed and avoided. At least by those in our set. Perhaps behaviors are different among the poor."

"Perhaps." He squeezed her arm. "I'm glad you like it here. The plains are remote, and the isolation isn't for everyone."

He pointed to a chunky bird running along the ground. Swathed in brown and cream bars, the bird had small wings and circular orange sacs on either side of its beak. "That's a male prairie chicken."

She squinted and shielded her eyes from the setting sun. "Does he have ears?"

"No." He chuckled. "Those are feathers. He can raise or lower them. And you should see him dance when it's time to attract a mate. Something to view, to be sure."

"Dancing chickens? Now I know I'm not in Baltimore anymore." She sent him a saucy grin. "What else have you got?"

"Bighorn sheep reside in the western part of the state." He winked. "Bet you don't see those in Maryland. Standing over three feet tall, they can weigh more than three hundred pounds, and their curved horns are huge. Elk too. You should hear the males when they get to bellowing. A sound you'll never forget."

"Aside from your chickens, are all Nebraska animals large?"

Nathan shook his head. "In fact, most are quite small. On another day, we'll take a field trip to the prairie-dog town."

"Wild dogs?" She licked her dry lips. Were they dangerous like some of the strays who roamed Baltimore's alleys?

"No, a bit of a misnomer. They're rodents. Related to squirrels, I think, but the sound they make is reminiscent of a dog's bark."

"Why is their home called a town?"

"They live in family groups and build colonies of burrows that can take up a large amount of ground. The entrances to the tunnels are mounded." The house came into view, and he leaned forward. "Today's educational tour is concluded. Please tip your driver as you exit the wagon."

Dinah laughed and jabbed Nathan, who responded with a grunt. She loved their time alone together. He was intelligent and funny, taking her mind of the niggling doubts that plagued her about her brothers. She sobered. If he discovered her identity, would he send her away? There was no reason to return to Baltimore. Would Lincoln reject her, too, or could she find a job that enabled her to stay? She sighed. Would she have to run from her past for the rest of her life?

⸻ ••◦●◦•• ⸻

Nathan took a deep breath, inhaling the scents that encompassed the prairie. Seeing Nebraska through the fresh eyes of Dinah was fun. Only eighteen months or so had passed since he'd taken up residence, but he was already taking for granted the expanse of land and the wildlife that called the plains home. If she enjoyed the chicken, the prairie dogs would surely amuse her. Maybe he'd put together a picnic and take Florence with them.

He sighed. Georgianna had never had the opportunity to experience this life. Images of his wife flashed through his head. Rocking Florence to sleep. Sitting by the fire stitching a quilt. Bent over the table kneading bread, a smudge of flour dusting her cheek. Tears pricked the backs of his eyes, and he swallowed the lump that had formed in his throat. Would he ever get to the point when he would stop missing Georgianna? No longer feel her absence as a gaping chasm in his gut?

Clinging to his sorrow was unfair to Dinah who had given up her life back east to marry him and care for Florence. Was he doing an injustice to his prospective bride to expect her to marry him when he didn't love her? Granted, he'd not promised to love her, but did she expect the sentiment to eventually grow? She deserved better than a grieving widow who couldn't give her his heart.

He licked his lips. Time to put a stop to the proceedings. A mail-order bride was not the right decision for him. Florence would be upset, but she'd soon forget Dinah. Only two weeks had passed since she'd entered their lives. Would she hate him for his rejection?

"Dinah—"

The sound of horses' hooves thundered across the field. He rose in the wagon, his eyes searching for the rider. In the distance, Jacob Muir raced toward them on the farm's black stallion, Midnight. He held the reins of a saddled, but riderless brown gelding. The animals' strides ate up the gap, soon drawing alongside them. Midnight's sides heaved, and he snorted. The gelding huffed out a breath. Jacob dragged his hat from his head. "Nate, I'm glad you're almost home. You must come quickly." He glanced at Dinah. "Immediately, if possible."

"What is it? Florence? Is she all right?"

"Yes, sir. It's not your daughter. We've got a difficult birth with one of the cows. We've done all we can to make her comfortable, but the calf refuses to be born. We're concerned about losing one or both of them."

"Have you tried pulling out the animal?"

"We were unsuccessful. The poor thing seems caught inside its mother."

Dinah gasped, and Nathan laid his hand on her shoulder. She was going to learn about the dark side of farm life. "I'll be there as soon—"

"Go." Dinah squeezed his hand. "Take the horse and head to the barn with Jacob. I'll bring the wagon. The distance is not that far, only a mile or so." She cocked her head. "And I can see the house from here, so I can't get lost."

"Are you sure? As you said, it's not far, so maybe I should finish driving you to the cabin."

"Nathan, every moment counts. I'll be praying that God sees fit to save your cow and her baby." She tugged the reins from his hand. "Now, go."

He looked at Jacob who nodded, then back to Dinah's earnest face. Her eyes were clear, her face determined. He cupped her cheek in his hand, and his chest lightened. "Thank you." He scrambled from the wagon and leapt onto the horse. With a wave, he turned the horse and was soon galloping toward the homestead.

How had he doubted his need of her in his life? No, he didn't love her, but she would make a strong and supportive partner. He would follow through with the agreement to marry her and pretend to care, so she would feel the love she deserved.

Dinah's Dilemma

Chapter Ten

A humid gust flapped the sheets Dinah hung on the line. The earlier cloudburst had only served to raise the level of humidity in the air. Sizzling on the ground as it fell, the rain hadn't permeated the packed ground. According to Nathan, the hot summer wasn't unexpected, but the lack of precipitation could be problematic if not resolved soon.

She plucked a clothespin from the pocket of her apron and wrestled a towel onto the rope. *Please, God, send the rains. Don't let Nathan's crops fail. He's worked hard to make a life here.* Her chest tightened. Was constant worry to be her lot?

Voices floated across the wind, and she peeked around the waving laundry.

Jacob Muir, the foreman, stood several yards away, his hat pushed back on his head and his arms crossed, talking to a stranger. Tall and lanky, the man slouched against his horse. Brim pulled low, his hat shadowed his features. His clothing was worn, but clean, and his boots scuffed.

Squinting against the sun's glare, she studied the man. Something in his stance seemed familiar, but everyone she knew in Nebraska lived or worked on the farm. She slid behind the sheet and strained to hear the conversation. Her mother would be horrified at her intentional eavesdropping.

"What kind of experience you got driving cattle?"

"A bunch. Last season I did two runs. One for the Bar M ranch, and one for the Triple Nine. Both from Texas."

"Texas, eh? What brings you to Nebraska?"

"I heard the money was better up here. More per head. Am I right?"

"Yep. Too many animals in Texas. Drove down the price."

"I'm willing to take any job you've got, not just moving cattle to market."

Dinah closed her eyes and wrapped her arms around her middle. The man's nasal twang grated in her ears. Foggy memories swirled. Her heart pounded. He claimed he was from Texas, but was the stranger really from Maryland? Is that why she recognized his speech? Or did she miss her homeland so acutely that she imagined a resemblance where there was none?

"I got no work at the moment. Crops are all planted, and we're keeping the boys busy working on maintenance. Try over at Barnard Johnson's place, the Double J. His spread is three times that of any other place close by."

"Thanks. Mind if I check back closer to cattle driving time?"

"Not at all, but I ain't making any promises."

"Understood."

Footsteps clomped toward Dinah, and she wrestled another towel onto the line. Putting what she hoped was a nonchalant expression on her face, she glanced up as the visitor walked past.

He tipped his head in acknowledgment then froze, his eyes wide. "I know you, don't I?" His gaze raked her face, his deep-set eyes, almost black in the shade of his hat. He took a step toward her, and a sneer twisted his face as recognition seemed to dawn in his expression. "You're Herbert's and Jerome's older sister, ain't you? I heard you'd left Baltimore, but I sure never expected to see you turn up out West. You was all tea parties and balls. How'd you end up on a farm?"

Her heart banged, threatening to leap from her chest. Perspiration broke out on her hairline, and her hands trembled. "How—?

"How I got here ain't important, but I sure would like to know what sort of snake oil you're selling."

"Selling?" Dinah's voice cracked. "I'm not selling anything."

He narrowed his eyes. "Did you tell these folks who you are? That you're tied to a gang back east? Too bad I couldn't finish the job I started."

Her vision swam, and she blinked. The man who attacked her as she was getting on the streetcar. She couldn't faint. Not now. Not while this man stood within earshot of the house, spouting her past. She straightened her spine and drew herself to her full height. "I'm afraid you have me confused with someone else. I've got work do to, so you best be on your way." Would he believe her bluff? Her lie? *God, help me!*

A harsh, ugly laugh split the air. "I see your fear." He strode toward her, a leer on his face. He gripped her arm and shook her. "I won't say nothing for the time being. You must have a good thing going here to be worried I'm gonna ruin all that. This is quite a spread, so the guy must have lots of money you're trying to get your hands on. But know this, I'll be back, and I'll want my cut."

"Hey! Let go of her!" Nathan raced toward them, his face dark with anger.

Dropping his hand as if scalded, the man moved away.

Dinah stumbled and fell in a heap on the ground, her breath ragged and uneven. Her stomach roiled, and she swallowed against the nausea that swept over her.

Nathan grabbed the man by the scruff of his neck and shoved him. "Who are you, and what do you think you're doing?"

"Nothing. Just a misunderstanding. Didn't mean nothing by it."

"I suggest you get off my property immediately. I don't take kindly to strangers manhandling my guests."

With slow motions, the man brushed off his coat and settled his hat on his head. He squared his shoulders and touched his brim in a two-fingered salute. "Yes, sir." His gaze riveted on Dinah, he lowered his left eyelid in an exaggerated wink. "Sorry for the mix-up, ma'am. Have a nice day."

He climbed on his horse, wheeled the animal around, and cantered toward the road.

Dinah cringed, her body trembling from head to toe. The past had come calling. Had Nathan heard any of their interaction? He'd been far off, but as she'd discovered, the wind could carry voices some distance.

Worry etched on his face, Nathan squatted in front of her. "Are you all right? Did he injure you? Did you get hurt when you fell?"

"No, but he frightened me." She shook her head. "I didn't know what to do."

"Fortunately, I saw what was happening when I came out of the barn. I think we can praise God for my intervention. I was supposed to be mending fences, but my horse threw a shoe."

Had God saved her? Was He watching out for her? Even in her sinful state?

Nathan held out his hands. "Can you try to stand?"

She nodded, blinking back tears.

He wrapped his arm around her shoulders and helped her to her feet. She swayed then collapsed against Nathan's firm chest. Should she ask him if he heard anything, or would her question raise suspicion? Living a lie was exhausting, but did she have a choice?

Dinah's Dilemma

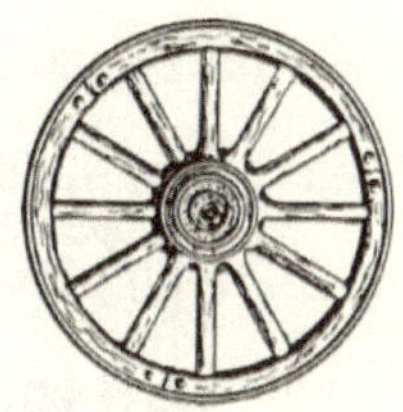

Chapter Eleven

Her fingers working of their own volition, Dinah shelled peas and watched Nathan break a new colt in the pen not far from the house. A chore she'd done even in Baltimore, the simple act of running her finger along each pod to release its tiny orbs with a clatter into the bowl was soothing. Her mind went back to days just like this one: sitting on a porch with a sun-filled sky and light breeze. She wrinkled her nose, however. Nebraska's smells of dirt, manure, and other earthy aromas were nothing like the pungent stink of coal and burning wood in Baltimore.

The horse whinnied and galloped away from Nathan, his neck arched and head held high. Sweat glistened on the animal's coat, reminiscent of melted chocolate. His eyes wide, he watched Nathan's every move.

Nathan had been working with the horse for more than an hour, yet Nathan's expression held no frustration, only a soft smile as he kept up a constant chatter. Praising the animal for his beauty and strong spirit, he walked with a relaxed gait. He periodically approached the animal and stroked its nose or sides.

About ten minutes ago, the horse had stopped throwing off the blanket that Nathan laid on his back. The saddle should come soon.

After shelling the last pod, Dinah massaged her aching fingers. She should go into the house to see what other chores needed to be done, but she was drawn to the activities in the corral. Nathan was in his element when he was gentling an animal. The man had the patience of Job, never once losing his temper. He seemed less intent on breaking the will of the animal and more on working out a partnership.

Her heart flip-flopped. Even in dirty, sweat-stained clothes, Nathan was a handsome man. His deep-blue eyes sparkled and crinkled at the edges as if he were having great fun. His muscles bunched and strained under his shirt. His hands were firm yet tender with the horse.

Behind her, the screen door banged. Mrs. Crowell lowered herself into the seat next to Dinah. She set a cup of water on the table between them then drank deeply from her own glass. "Too warm in the house, but not much better out here. I thought you could use some refreshment."

"Thank you." Dinah took a sip then held the glass in her lap. "The heat here is different than in Baltimore. The macadam radiates the temperature against the buildings which block most of the breeze, whereas here, the wind blows free."

"I lived in Chicago for a while. Too many people in the city for my taste, so I came West. Mr. Childs is the third family I've kept house for. He's been the most kind of all of them."

"He is a gracious man." Dinah's gaze was drawn to the brawny figure in the pen. "Even with his animals."

"And with you."

"Yes." Dinah's cheeks warmed. But not gracious enough to move forward with the wedding.

Mrs. Crowell took another swallow of water then cleared her throat. "You've been here nearly a month and seem to be settling in."

"Three weeks and one day."

"But who's counting?" Mrs. Crowell snickered. "Most couples set a date if they don't marry upon the girl's arrival. Not really any of my business, but you two don't seem in a hurry to wed."

"You'll need to discuss the situation with Nathan. This is his farm and his plan. I'm quite willing to move forward with the wedding. He's indicated a desire to get to know each other prior to getting married."

"How long's that going to take?" The housekeeper cocked her head. "Granted, there's plenty of staff on site, but aren't you worried about your reputation, living here without being hitched?"

Dinah shrugged. "I learned a long time ago not to rearrange my life on the basis of what others thought about me. Oftentimes, they don't know the whole story before weighing in with their opinions, so I find it better to determine my own course of action."

"That's a rather…uh…modern…way of thinking."

"I'm sorry if I've offended you, Mrs. Crowell." Dinah rubbed her forehead. Did the woman blame her for the lack of a wedding? "But as I said, Nathan seems in no hurry to culminate the arrangement. Perhaps you should be having this conversation with him. After all, you've known him longer than I."

"I'm not insulted, just surprised, although I guess I shouldn't be. Took several months before Sheriff Denard could convince Mr. Childs to contact the agency."

"I'm beginning to believe he rues that decision." Dinah plucked at her skirt, rolling the fabric between her fingers. "His late wife is still very much a part of him. I don't believe he'll ever get over her enough to let another woman into his heart. They must have had a very special love."

Mrs. Crowell patted her arm. "I didn't know his wife. He came to Nebraska after her death. But from what I see, love isn't what's holding him back. It's guilt. In some corner of his soul, he believes he's responsible for her death. That she wouldn't have died if he wasn't with the Pinkertons. He may not want to risk that sort of thing happening again. To love and then lose because of himself." She sipped from the glass.

"He's a farmer now. How could he put me in danger?"

"Perhaps that's the conversation you should have with him."

Dinah stared across the expanse of corn tassels waving. Nathan wasn't the only one fighting feelings of guilt. She'd failed to tell him of her brothers' gang activities knowing he would probably reject her if he knew. The information would invariably surface, the timing a matter of when, not if. She should leave before either she or Florence got any more attached to each other. Her heart stuttered. Nathan's daughter wasn't the only person on the farm she'd miss.

⸺ ••••⚙•••• ⸺

Head against the horse's neck, Nathan breathed in the scent of leather, sweat, and soil. The colt had done well today. No need to push him further. Tomorrow was soon enough to convince him to wear the saddle. Maybe only a few more days until they could ride together.

"Good boy." He stroked the animal's shoulder then rubbed his nose.

The horse nickered and bobbed his head as if agreeing with the assessment.

Nathan gestured to the farmhand, who leaned against the rails watching the activity. No matter how docile a horse appeared, breaking an animal alone was never wise. The youngest of his men, the lad had stood alert, ready to intervene if anything went wrong. "Please give him a rubdown and some extra oats. He worked hard today."

"Yes, sir." The boy grabbed the reins and led the horse out of the corral, murmuring as he walked. With his love of his horses, the young man would make a good stable master someday.

His mouth dry, Nathan ran his tongue across his lips to moisten them. A dousing under the pump was in order. He turned and froze. Dinah and Mrs. Crowell sat on the porch staring in his direction. How long had they been watching? He squinted and tried to read Dinah's expression, a mixture of emotions warring for supremacy. Was something wrong?

He picked up his hat and banged off the dust against his thigh then plopped it on his head. The pump could wait. He hurried toward the house, heart banging in his chest, but not from the exertion of breaking the horse. Would Dinah be pleased with what he'd done?

"You ladies enjoying the sunshine?" He leaned against the post. "Or just supervising my work?"

Dinah blushed a lovely shade of pink and ducked her head.

Mrs. Crowell smirked. "A little of both, Mr. Childs. You're making good progress with that colt. Shouldn't be long before he's carrying you across the plains."

"He's smart as a whip. And he seems eager to please."

"Because you make him want to do so." Dinah's voice was soft, nearly a whisper. "He loves you already."

Nathan's chest swelled, and he fought the urge to shuffle his toe against the floorboard like a schoolboy, but her praise meant a lot to him. He smiled. "Nah, it's the extra oats."

"You're incorrigible, Mr. Childs. Take a compliment as it's given."

"Yes, Mrs. Crowell." He executed an exaggerated bow at his housekeeper, matching her smirk with one of his own.

She snorted a laugh and rose. Lifting her glass from the table, she gestured to her vacant seat. "Take a rest, and I'll bring you some water."

"Thanks." He dropped into the chair and stretched out his legs. The day had started early. He pushed his hat back on his head. "I've got a surprise for you."

Dinah's face lit up, and she bolted upright. "A surprise?"

He chuckled. "Yes. You seem to be holding up pretty good with the isolation, but I figured you get lonely for other ladies. Mrs. Crowell is one of my employees, nice enough, but not exactly a friend, so I've invited Sheriff Denard and his wife, Livvy over for dinner tonight."

"Tonight?" Dinah's hand flew to her throat. "How soon?"

"Dunno. Couple of hours, I guess. I kind of lost track of time working with the colt. Mrs. Crowell knows about it, so she's got the meal well in hand, I'm sure. Your only job is to put on one of those new outfits you made and do your hair. Not that you don't look pretty right now…uh, but don't you gals like to get dressed up?"

"Yes, I like to wear nice things." Her cheeks reddened again. "I hope you don't think me vain."

"Never." He crossed his arms. "You and Livvy seemed to get on well at the social, so I thought you'd enjoy more time with her, and I wouldn't mind seeing Alfred again."

Her smile froze, and her gaze clouded.

That happened often when he talked about the sheriff. What was it about the man that caused such a strong reaction? Sure, he was a tough lawman, but he had a soft spot for the ladies and went out of his way to take care of them. Was her response one of fear? If so, what was she afraid of? When she got like this, guarded—a haunted look in her eyes—his investigative senses itched as if there was more to her than she was telling. What had happened to make her so skittish?

"Listen, Dinah. I appreciate your patience with me…about not proposing or asking you to set a date for the wedding. I don't want you to regret your decision to come to Nebraska. To marry me. I want you to be happy here." He shoved his hands into his pockets and hunched his shoulders. "But would you be willing to give me a little more time?"

With enough time, perhaps he could solve her problem—whatever it was.

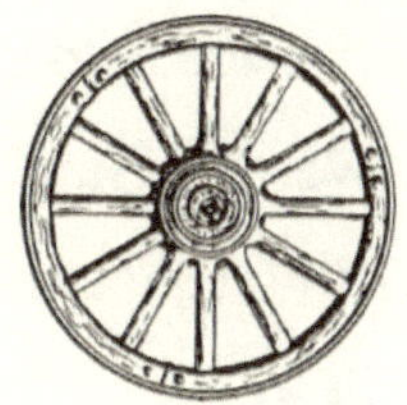

Chapter Twelve

Silverware clinked on china, and Dinah wiped her mouth on the cloth napkin. The sheriff and his wife sat across from her and Nathan, and every time she looked up, the lawman seemed to be studying her. Had he discovered her identity? Was he waiting for the perfect time to make the announcement or would he hold the information over her head and expect something in exchange for silence? Mrs. Crowell volunteered to feed Florence, so the little girl was not present to create the desired distraction.

"That's a beautiful dress, Dinah." Livvy smiled. "Did you make it yourself?"

"Uh, yes. Thank you. Mama insisted that I learn sewing, and the skill has come in handy."

"Especially when you've got to stitch up your man here." Sheriff Denard winked. "Never knew him to be so clumsy before."

Nathan flushed. "Funny, Alfred. I can talk about more than a few times you were less than steady on your feet."

"Yeah, okay. I'll quit ribbing you." The sheriff leaned his elbows on the table. "Problem is, Miss Reinhardt, Nathan and I go way back. We know where each other's skeletons are hidden."

Dinah's heart thudded. Was he insinuating he knew about her skeletons? She licked her lips and forced a smile. "Then we'll have to spend some time together, won't we?"

He slapped the table and laughed. "I'd like that."

"Let them keep some of the mystery alive." Livvy poked her husband. "Have you and Nathan set a date, Dinah?"

"Not yet, but we're talking about it." She glanced at Nathan whose jaw tightened. "I understand you were a mail-order bride. Not to pry, but your marriage seems to have worked out well."

Livvy nodded and rubbed the sheriff's arm. "It hasn't been all sunshine and roses, but we love each other deeply." A shadow crossed her face. "I was engaged back east, in Boston, but my fiancé proved to be less than honorable, so I called off the wedding. Very few believed what I knew to be true, so I was ostracized, shunned from society for bringing embarrassment to him. My friend was a client of Mrs. Crenshaw's and suggested I apply. Alfred and I wrote letters for a while, getting to know each other. He proposed after six months. We married as soon as I arrived."

"But you had problems?" Dinah frowned. "Do you mind telling me what happened?"

"I had trouble adjusting to the life of a lawman's wife. He's in constant danger, and the hours aren't exactly regular. I felt like he was putting the job before me, but through the counsel of a very wise woman here in town, I realized my fears were unfounded."

"Who—"

"The widow of the former sheriff."

"Widow?" Dinah cocked her head.

Livvy shook her head. "Sheriff Chambers lived to a ripe old age."

"I'm glad Nathan has given up being a Pinkerton agent." Dinah blew out a breath. "Having him gone a lot and at risk would be difficult for me."

"You'd miss me?" Nathan waggled his eyebrows.

"She might, but I'd get along okay." Sheriff Denard forked a piece of steak into his mouth. "Of course, you'd miss me. That's why you came to Lincoln. 'Cause I'm here."

"Seemed like a good idea at the time. Now, I'm beginning to regret my decision."

"Cute." The sheriff stabbed a potato chunk. "Florence seems to be doing well. She was real perky when I came in tonight."

"Dinah must have had a lot to do with that." Livvy laid down her fork. "You were a teacher back east, right?"

"I haven't done much. She was a delightful child already. Outgoing and curious."

"Nathan says you've been teaching her to read." Sheriff Denard cocked his head. "Isn't she a bit young?"

Dinah shrugged. "I hadn't plan to get her started, but when I read to her, she'd point to the words and ask what they were. She wanted to follow along. I've never worked with a student this age, but she seems to be picking up the knowledge quite well."

Nathan pushed away his empty plate. "Florence is blooming under Dinah's care. And has grown to love her."

"How sweet." Livvy beamed. "And you must love her, too."

"Yes." Dinah's chest tightened. She did love Florence, and she would miss her desperately. "Would anyone care for coffee? Mrs. Crowell made a cake."

"Alfred and I need to check on something in the barn. How about if you get dessert cut and served? We won't be long."

Livvy's eyes narrowed. "This can't wait?"

"I don't mean to be rude, Livvy, but it's important."

She raised one eyebrow, her lips thin. "Then take your time. We ladies have plenty to talk about."

Nathan and the sheriff rose and hurried out the door into the night.

Dinah exchanged glances with Livvy, then climbed to her feet, and began to clear the soiled dishes. Livvy joined her, and they went into the kitchen. She rinsed and stacked the plates then dumped the silverware into a pot.

"I'll cut the cake, Dinah, if you'll take care of the coffee."

"Sure, but you're the guest. I can handle both."

"The boys will take longer than they claim, so I don't plan to wait for them."

"But—"

"This isn't proper society. They can join us when they return."

Moments later, she was seated at the kitchen table next to the sheriff's wife.

Livvy squeezed Dinah's hand. "I'm sensing some reticence from you. Are things okay between you and Nathan? Will you be setting a date or heading home?"

Dinah widened her eyes. "Uh—"

"Alfred would tell me I'm being nosy and intrusive, but I've grown to like you, Dinah, and I don't want to see you get hurt. Nathan either. Would you like to talk? I'm a willing listener."

Tears threatened, and Dinah blinked away the moisture. Her shoulders sagged. "Even though she's not lived here, Nathan's wife is everywhere. He thinks about her constantly." Her lower lip trembled. "And I can tell he doesn't think I measure up."

"Have you discussed your concerns with Nathan?"

Dinah shook her head.

"Marriage isn't easy, but communication is crucial to success." Livvy sipped some coffee. "As believers, we agree that God guides our steps, right? Do you think He arranged to have you come to Nebraska?"

"Yes, Mrs. Crenshaw's presence was not coincidence. But maybe He doesn't plan for us to marry. Maybe I'm here for some other reason."

"That's possible, but I see the way you and Nathan look at each other when you don't think anyone notices. You both care. Your feelings may not be love yet, but there are embers that could be flamed." Livvy leaned forward and laid her hand on Dinah's arm. "Have you prayed about God's plan? Are you listening for His voice in all this?"

"Probably not in the way you mean. I've been talking to Him, but—"

"Telling Him what you think He should do?" Livvy smiled. "I do that sometimes."

Dinah's face warmed. "Yes. And complaining, too. Thank you for your friendship, Livvy. For caring enough to speak to me about this."

"Us gals have to stick together." She picked up her fork. "You've got to give me Mrs. Crowell's recipe. This cake is divine."

"She—"

Footsteps clomped outside.

"I said I'd get back to you. Stop pestering me." The sheriff's voice was muffled.

The door swung open, and Dinah's gaze whipped toward the men whose expressions were a mixture of annoyance and guilt.

What topic of conversation would produce such looks on their faces? Would Nathan tell her if she asked?

Chapter Thirteen

Standing next to Dinah, Nathan lifted his hand in farewell as Alfred's wagon pulled away from the house. A wide smile on her face, Livvy waved with both arms high over her head. He couldn't ask for better friends, and Alfred couldn't have found a better wife. Warm and friendly, Livvy exuded love in every circumstance. Even when she'd reprimanded him for taking Alfred to the barn before dessert, she'd meant the correction for his good.

The sun dipped toward the horizon, sending shards of orange, purple, and pink across the cobalt sky. Ever present, the breeze brushed his cheeks and ruffled his hair. Nearly ready to harvest, the wheat swayed and danced in the evening light. From the barn, the cows mooed, and the horses nickered as they settled in for the night. Bats swooped overhead, dining on dusk's first mosquitos.

He blew out a deep breath, contentment filling his chest. "A nice visit with Alfred and Livvy, don't you think?"

She smiled, her face partially shadowed. "Yes. Livvy has been wonderful, treating me as if we were old friends."

"That's her way. She's never met a stranger and having been a newcomer herself, she goes out of her way to be welcoming. Alfred is lucky to have her. She softens his rough edges."

"Thank you for inviting them over. I've been busy enough not to realize I was lonely, but their visit had made me feel like a saturated flower after the rain. Full and satisfied."

"I'm glad." He shrugged. "I get caught up in doing the work that I forget to have fun. You may have to remind me occasionally, but I'll do my best to remember."

"Speaking of work, I need to get the washing off the line." She turned toward the rope filled with laundry. "See you inside."

Nathan hurried after her. "I promised to help. After all, I'm the one who asked you to leave it for later. It's later."

Dinah grinned, eyes sparkling. "You're right. This is your fault." She unpinned a sheet.

He chuckled and grabbed one end of the cloth. They folded the fabric lengthwise then he walked toward her to fold the sheet in half. Dinah collected his portion, her fingers grazing his. A jolt shot up his arms as if he'd been struck by lightning during a summer storm.

Heart thumping, he watched as she doubled the sheet before dropping it in the basket on the ground. She unpinned another sheet, and they started the process over. Nathan braced himself for the feel of her fingers on his hands. Her feather-soft touch sent tingles to his chest.

Why had he initially thought her plain? In addition to her beautiful spirit, her appearance was delicate and refined, her complexion clear and fair. Chocolate-brown eyes sparked with intelligence. Her new dress hugged her comely figure in all the right places.

"Thank you for all you're doing to make our house a home, Dinah. The chores can be somewhat tedious, but you do them with a cheerful heart, and I appreciate that."

Her cheeks pinked in the fading light, and she shrugged. "No more so than your tasks. And spending time with Florence is never tedious."

"Anything but. My girl is a handful, but she minds you."

"She's learned there's a time for work and a time for fun."

"But you make her work enjoyable, a game."

"Yes, my mother taught me that way." She sighed and dropped another sheet into the basket.

"You must miss her very much. We could arrange for you to visit or bring her here to see you."

Dinah shook her head, her lips thin. "No, Mother is needed in Baltimore. You are very generous, but maybe another time."

They fell silent, unpinning and folding the sheets in a comfortable rhythm. The sun nipped the horizon by the time they finished. Nathan gripped the basket and headed toward the house. "Would you like to sit on the porch for a bit?"

"Tempting, but I've still got mending to finish."

His stomach fell. "Surely, there's nothing in the stack of importance."

"No, mostly darning. Truth be told, mending socks isn't my most proficient skill, so I tend to put off the task."

Nathan nudged her shoulder. "Well, if it will help, I'll purchase a large supply of socks the next time we're in town, then you won't have to worry about them."

She giggled and shook her head. "Nonsense, that's extravagant."

He smiled. "All right, but the offer holds."

"Thank you, kind sir." Dinah bobbed in an exaggerated curtsy. "I'll remember that when my fingers are tired and calloused.

They entered the house, and he carried the basket to the cedar-lined cherrywood chest near the stairs. He set it on the floor, and she opened the lid of the trunk, the smoky scent filling his nose. He closed his eyes for a brief moment. A wedding gift, he'd almost left the cabinet behind when he moved, but the furniture was practical in its ability to stave off moths.

Dinah knelt and tucked the linens into one side of the chest. She pulled out a pile of butter-yellow napkins. "I'm ready for a change, and these are just the ticket. A yummy color." More digging, and she tugged on the corner of a quilt buried in the bottom. "This looks pretty. Perhaps I'll change the cover on the bed, if you don't mind." She flushed and looked at him with concern. "The bedroom is yours."

"Not right now. I'm sleeping in the barn, remember?"

"You know what I mean." She shifted the sheets until she uncovered the patchwork spread. Stroking the multicolored design, she smiled. "Gorgeous. Such intricate work. I've never attempted a quilt."

He froze and stared at the fabric in her hand, dizziness threatening to overtake him. His wedding quilt. But it couldn't be. Steeped in pain after the funeral, he'd tossed the spread, as well as Georgianna's clothes and personal items, into a pile of goods being donated to the needy. Had the pastor's wife somehow returned the spread? Why would she do that?

"Put that away." Nathan's voice was cold as steel. "I don't want to see it."

"What?" Confusion etched lines in Dinah's face. "The quilt is beautiful and should be on display."

"Do as I tell you, and stuff that thing back where you found it." A lead ball settled in his chest. "Or bury it. I don't care which you do."

"But—"

"Now," he roared then grabbed the quilt from her hands and shoved it to the bottom of the chest. With frantic motions, he dumped the remaining linen on top of the offending material. His vision swirled, and he swayed. Putting his hand to the wall, he steadied himself.

Her face paled, and tears trickled down her cheeks. "I'm sorry." Barely a whisper, her voice cracked. Trembling, she rose and stepped back, her eyes wide and frightened.

"Dinah—"

She shook her head and backed away from him, hands fluttering. "I'm sorry," she repeated. "I didn't mean to offend you. I'll retire for the night." She whirled and rushed toward the bedroom, slipping inside, and closing the door with a thud.

But not before he saw her face. Eyes clouded, skin ashen and damp with tears, her face was raw with pain. What had he done?

Oh Lord, forgive me.

He hurried to the door and knocked. "Dinah, I'm sorry. I was awful." He swallowed past the lump in his throat. "Please forgive me."

Silence.

"Dinah?"

"Please go away." Her voice was muffled. "I'd like to be alone, if you don't mind."

"I understand." His shoulders slumped, and he rubbed his throbbing forehead. Seeing the quilt had ripped open his grief, overwhelming him, and pushing him into the dark abyss of loss and despair. He blew out a shaky sigh. And he'd spewed his anger and misery onto Dinah. Sweet Dinah.

What could he do to salve the hurt he'd inflicted?

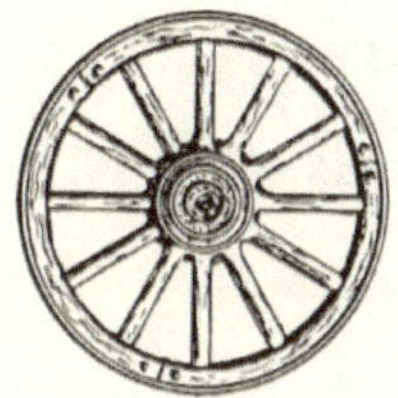

Chapter Fourteen

Dinah bolted upright in the bed. She'd fallen on the mattress fully clothed, stifling the sound of her cries in the pillow. At some point, fatigue had overtaken her, and she slept. But now, the sound of hammering pounded overhead. What was happening?

She leapt up and ran to the window. Darkness encompassed the world outside. Then lightning flashed. Hail, and sheets of rain pummeled the ground. Thunder rumbled. More lightning. Her heart beat in rhythm with the steady banging of the ice balls on the roof. She pressed her palms against her ears. The rain was a gift, but what would the hail do to the crops?

Behind her, the bedroom door swung open. Eyes wide and his face lined with worry, Nathan stood in the doorway.

She pulled down her arms and wrapped them around her waist.

He beckoned her toward him. "Step away from the window. The ice could break the glass."

"Oh, of course." Her voice trembled as she walked to him. He'd think her a coward.

"Have you experienced a hailstorm before?"

"Not like this. Tiny beads of ice sometimes, but nothing larger." She shivered. "The horses and cows?"

"Already safe in the barn. They're nervous, so a couple of the boys are with them."

Dinah nodded then licked her lips. She knew exactly how the animals felt. But who would calm her fears? "Uh, thank you for checking on me."

Nathan reached for her then dropped his hand. "Dinah, please forgive my outburst earlier. My behavior was unconscionable." He pressed his hands to his chest, his face red, and his eyes uncertain. "I have so much anger bottled up inside, and sometimes the emotion erupts, and I say and do things…"

"I understand. You must have loved her very much." He would never love her as deeply, if at all. She slumped. "No need to apologize."

"I have every reason to apologize, and I hope you'll forgive me." A sheen of moisture covered his eyes, and he blinked. "You've been very gracious in waiting for me to be ready to remarry."

She kneaded her fingers and shrugged. How should she respond?

His gaze moved to her knotted hands, and his forehead creased. "Are you frightened? Would you like me to keep you company until the storm passes?"

Another shrug. Would he believe her attempt at nonchalance?

He closed the distance between them and drew her to him, his arms warm and comforting. He rubbed circles on her back and murmured in her ear.

Tingles enveloped her, and she sagged against his firm, safe form. His heart beat steady and sure against her cheek. A sigh escaped. "You must think me foolish to be afraid of the weather."

"Not at all." Nathan released her and tipped up her chin until their eyes met. "Weather in Nebraska is extreme and can be dangerous, changing in a moment. A healthy respect for the elements is wise." He laced her fingers in his and tugged. "Let's wait out the storm on the sofa with tea and cookies. Sound good?"

"Yes." She huffed out a deep breath. "Thank you for not laughing at my…concerns."

"Never." His gaze raked her face. "I would not do such a thing."

They left the bedroom, and Dinah put water in the kettle and lit the stove. Nathan laid several oatmeal cookies onto a platter then pulled out a pair of teacups. He put the plate on the table by the couch then prowled the room, hands in his pockets, occasionally peeking out the window at the tempest. The pot finally whistled, and she poured hot water over the tea leaves, the fragrant floral steam filling her senses.

He came to the kitchen, and Dinah handed him his cup, her fingers skimming his. She quivered and ducked her head. Why couldn't her body understand that she couldn't fall in love with him?

In the living room, they sank onto the sofa. Dinah sipped her tea, her ears cocked against the thumping outside. On the roof. On the porch. Against the windows. She hunkered down in the cushions.

Nathan set down his cup and crossed his legs. "Let's get our mind off the storm. Tell me more about Maryland. What did you love about it? The state doesn't have hail like this, so what is the weather like?"

She took another drink from her cup. "I thought you'd been to Maryland."

"Yes, but I want to see it through your eyes. I was on duty most of the time."

"Okay." She gazed at the fireplace, wood set but unlit. "We lived in the city, but when I was a young girl, Father would take us to the Chesapeake Bay. We would picnic and sometimes ride one of the boats. Crabbing was my favorite."

"Crabbing?"

"Catching blue crabs. We'd attached fish parts to a string that was tied to the post on the pier, then wait. Didn't usually take long to catch enough for a good meal." She smiled at the memory of her father, crab in hand, chasing her squealing mother. "Then the war came, and after the war, Father's…uh…difficulties began, so we stopped going."

"About your Father…I'm sorry for what happened."

"Me too. Maybe if we'd never had the happier times, life would have been easier. I'd have known how to handle his moods and behaviors."

"Perhaps, but I'm pleased you have good times to remember. Hopefully, they'll serve to buoy you when you get sad." He squeezed her hand. "His choices were unfortunate, and if I know Baltimore society, your family did not fare well once his deeds came to light. But you are here now, at the beginning of a fresh start."

The tightness in her chest eased. "Thank you for not judging me for my stepfather's actions."

"That would be unfair of me. Each person is responsible for their own choices. You shouldn't be penalized for his misdeeds. And he might not be able to help himself. We have not walked in his shoes." He stroked the back of her hand with his thumb. "I read an article last year by a doctor who has speculated that people who can't stop gambling suffer the same as those who crave liquor. Something inside them provokes the desire that can only be quenched at the gaming tables."

Her eyes widened. "I've never thought of his gambling that way. If what the doctor says is true, I should feel sorry for him, rather than angry."

He nodded. "Only God can break the chains of gambling that have trapped your father. We should pray for him. That someone enters his life to help."

Tears gathered in her eyes, and her chin trembled. "Yes, but I'm so angry. He ruined our family's reputation. Lost our money, and put us in dire straits. He should suffer for what he did, shouldn't he?"

"But that is not for us to judge, only God. In a world that is fair and just, your father would pay for the sorrow he's caused, but hard as it may be, we should ask for mercy instead."

Her lips twisted. "Then you should pray for me because I'm not sure I can beseech God on his behalf at this time."

"I understand, and I already do pray for you, so I will add this request to the list." He rubbed his forehead. "But I should ask for your intervention as well. Despite my advice about your father, I, too, have been withholding forgiveness." His grip on her hand tightened.

Her pulse raced. Was he upset with her? Had she done something to offend him?

Nathan cleared his throat. "I told you about the fire that took my wife, and the gang members I believe are responsible, but I failed to mention the attempts I made to find the guilty parties. I pulled together a posse to hunt down the men. We managed to get word of their whereabouts because they were foolish enough to brag about their deeds in a bar. Known for causing trouble, the barkeep notified the local authorities who passed along the information. We tracked them to Catonsville, then on to Ellicott City, but lost them on the way to Columbia."

Dinah stilled, her lower lip caught between her teeth. He listed all but one of the towns her brothers frequented. Was it a coincidence?

"We caught and arrested two members of the Bloody Tubs, but they alibied out and wouldn't give up their cohorts."

"The Bloody Tubs?" Her breathing hitched. "They were responsible for your wife's death?"

"Yes." His face darkened. "The night of the fire I vowed to kill the men responsible, but I no longer have that desire. But I do want to see justice served."

A chill swept over her. "They would hang if caught."

"But thus far, the Simpkins brothers have proven elusive."

Her stomach roiled. *Dear God, not Jerome and Herbert. They are not capable of murder. There must be a mistake.* But in her heart, she knew there was no error. Nathan would never marry her when he found out her relationship with his wife's killers. She must flee. Immediately.

Dinah's Dilemma

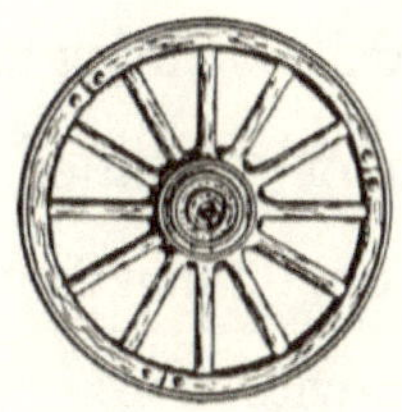

Chapter Fifteen

Early morning light seeped through the windows as Dinah stood in front of the stove frying ham and eggs. Her mouth watered, and her stomach rumbled in anticipation of the succulent, salty meat.

The front door opened, and Nathan came into the house. He'd changed his clothes, and his hair was slicked back. He walked behind her to the cabinet and pulled out two plates and a pair of mugs. "Smells good in here."

His musky scent mingling with the smell of lye soap assailed her. She could say the same thing. Last night's conversation came crashing back, and she shook her head. Mustn't get close. She forced a smile. "Food shouldn't be much longer, but the coffee's done."

"Perfect." He yawned and rotated his neck. "Today promises to be a long one. The boys are already in the fields doing cleanup. I took a quick ride around the perimeter, and we've got our work cut out for us."

"What can I do?"

"Keep Florence inside. The ground is muddy and slippery."

"I'd like to do more."

He gazed at her for a long moment, then a slow smile lit his face. "Regular deliveries of water and something to eat would be mighty helpful. We'll be putting out a lot of exertion."

Her breath hitched. "I can do that, and Florence will help. She needs to learn how to be a farmwife, too."

"Don't let her get out of the wagon."

"Understood." She grinned. "But I may have to strap her on board."

"I've no doubt." He chuckled and raised his mug. "But I think you're up to the task."

Dinah flipped the ham steaks, and the cast-iron skillet sizzled. She speared them onto their plates then scooped the creamy scrambled eggs out of the second pan. Bending, she pulled the golden-brown biscuits from the oven and dumped them into a waiting basket.

"You've outdone yourself this morning."

Her face warmed. "No more than usual."

"Considering what time we fell asleep, I'd say it is."

Memories of his gentle words and encouragement flooded her mind, warring with her thoughts of needing to leave before he discovered her despicable secret. She handed him his plate. Her fingers brushed his, and she shivered.

"Cold?"

"Uh, no. Not too much."

They sat at the table, and Nathan prayed a quick blessing over the food. Grateful he'd forgotten, or perhaps chose not to hold her hands during the prayer, Dinah forked a bite of eggs into her mouth. They ate in silence, the only sound in the room the clink of their silverware on the china plates.

Satiated, she set down her utensils and pushed away her plate. "Thank you for what you said about my father. It won't be easy, but I plan to work on forgiving him. God has convicted me of my own…uh…shortcomings."

"Good for you." His voice rumbled, warm and soothing. He sipped from the mug. "Then unless you wish to discuss the situation further, I won't say another word."

She nodded. "What will you do first this morning?"

"I'll work with Jacob to ascertain the extent of the damage. The boys will take care of the animals and any repairs needed as a result of the hail. I haven't seen ice balls this big before. Who knows what has been broken." He rubbed his face. "I pray we haven't sustained much crop loss."

"That would be worse than anything."

He smiled, fatigue bracketing his eyes. "You're learning. I can fix just about anything except wheat that's been beaten down. Hopefully, our neighbors haven't suffered too badly."

Dinah rose and cleared their soiled dishes. He was a good man. A farm full of potential problems, yet his thoughts went out to the other farmers. She didn't deserve him, but the storm meant she'd be unable to leave today. There would be no acceptable excuse to head to town and leave Florence in the care of Mrs. Crowell again. Her escape would have to wait one more day…or two.

Her pulse skittered. Better enjoy the happy times while she had them.

Nathan grabbed his Stetson from the stand by the door and plunked the hat on his head. "Thanks again for breakfast. Should hold me for a long while."

She wrapped the remaining biscuits in a towel and handed the warm package to him. "Here. You can use these more than I can."

"I won't turn you down." He winked and touched his brim in salute.

The door swung open, and Dinah jumped.

Sheriff Denard stood on the porch with the preacher by his side. His expression was terse.

Heart pounding, Dinah backed against the sink. Why was he here? Had he discovered her identity and assumed she was as guilty as her brothers? Would he try to arrest her? Her vision swirled, and she pressed her hands against her stomach. Her breakfast threatened to reappear.

"To what do we owe the pleasure for this early morning visit, Alfred?" Nathan dipped his head, his face wary. "Preacher, good to see you."

"Mind if we come in?"

"Uh, no." Nathan stepped back and gestured for the men to enter. He removed his hat and clutched it between his fingers. He turned to Dinah. "Any coffee left?"

"I'll check."

"Don't bother." The sheriff's voice was stern. At least, not yet."

"Now, you're scaring me, Alfred. What's going on? Something happen in town?"

"You could say that."

Dinah blinked and scrubbed at her face. Her mother would be horrified at her lack of manners. She took a deep breath. *Lord, help me deal with whatever situation the sheriff has brought.* "Sheriff, Pastor Youst, please have a seat."

Alfred removed his hat and clumped to the kitchen table where he dropped into one of the chairs. The preacher sat across from him.

Nathan rushed to Dinah and wrapped his arm around her shoulder, drawing her into one of the vacant seats. He sat beside her. "Okay, Alfred. Give us the news."

"I was going to come out last night, but then we had a bit of a punch-up in one of the saloons. By the time we got the varmints taken care of, the storm came. Didn't want to subject my horse or me to a long ride being pelted by ice balls."

Lips pinched, Nathan leaned forward. "Get to the point, Denard. I'm under the impression you don't really want to say what you've got to say."

Pastor Youst held up his hands. "What we've got to tell you is upsetting, but necessary." He glanced at Alfred who nodded. "Part of the reason for last night's…uh…incident is Miss Reinhardt here. Over the last few days, we've been hearing innuendoes about her living out here without the benefit of marriage. Her reputation is that she is a fast and loose woman."

Dinah gasped, and her hand flew to her mouth. Tears welled in her eyes. "But that's not fair. We've done nothing wrong." Apparently, Lincoln was no better than Baltimore with regard to maligning a person's character. She couldn't escape wagging tongues, no matter how far she traveled.

Nathan's face darkened, and he slammed his fist on the table. "Who is saying these odious untruths?"

"More than a few people." Pastor Youst laid his hand on Nathan's arm. "And despite the fact that their comments are malicious gossip, the damage to Miss Reinhardt's reputation has been done."

"This is nonsense. I'm sleeping in the barn with a half-dozen farmhands who will attest to that fact. Dinah and Florence sleep in the house. Nothing untoward has happened."

Alfred shook his head. "Doesn't matter. People's perception is all that matters. We can't have Miss Reinhardt thought of in this manner." His piercing gaze swept over Nathan then rested on Dinah. "You need to marry. Today. That's why the preacher is here. A couple of the hands or Jacob and Mrs. Crowell can act as witnesses."

Mouth gaping like a fish striving for air, Dinah pressed her hands over her eyes. So much for escaping before Nathan could find out about her brothers.

Nathan stroked her arm and bent close to her ear. "Getting married today is for the best, Dinah."

She dropped her hands to her lap and shook her head. "I could move into town. We could court properly. Or maybe I should leave Lincoln. Your reputation has suffered as well. The sooner I leave, the sooner I'll be forgotten."

He glared at Alfred and Pastor Youst. "Would you gentlemen give us a few moments?"

They clattered to their feet and hurried to the door. Alfred donned his hat. "We'll be right outside."

Nathan scooted his chair close to Dinah and clasped her fingers in his, stroking the back of her hand with small circles.

She hunched into herself. Why did he have to be so gentle and caring? So handsome.

He licked his lips. "I don't want you to leave. The situation is unfortunate, but you came here as a prospective bride, and I should have married you long before now. The damage to you is my fault. I'm sorry."

"We both decided to wait." She drew in a shaky breath. "You can't take all the blame."

"I'd like Florence to be part of the ceremony. Take your time getting prepared. We may not have planned to wed today, but there's no reason why the event can't be special. Alfred and Pastor Youst can wait as long as necessary until you're ready." He lifted her chin until her gaze met his. "Dinah, this will be a marriage in name only, until you decide to change that. I respect you a great deal and don't want to force you into…uh…relations you don't want."

She closed her eyes. *I don't understand Your plans, Lord, but I will trust You and go through with this. Is it selfish to ask that Nathan never finds out about my brothers?*

Chapter Sixteen

As if celebrating the upcoming nuptials, the sun shone bright in the morning sky. Nathan raked his fingers through his hair. His boots made sucking noises in the mud as he strode toward the barn to saddle Cinnamon. Reflections glittered in the puddles dotting the property.

Mrs. Crowell indicated he had plenty of time to gather the hands for the ceremony. She'd made it clear that the men could take time from storm repair to attend this most important event. Florence had squealed and clapped her hands, announcing she would act as flower girl. He smiled at her joyous expression. She'd grown to love Dinah and had blossomed under her care.

He entered the barn. Jacob looked up from collecting fence-mending tools. "Hey, boss. I'll have your supplies ready in a jiff."

"No hurry." Nathan stuffed his hands in his pockets and shuffled his feet. "There's been a slight change in plans."

Jacob's eyebrows shot up. Next to the crops, secure fencing was the most important part of the ranch side of his business. "You want me to get one of the other boys to handle this task?"

"Maybe. I'll decide that later. I need you to ride out to the east and south sections the property and collect the men. Tell 'em to get back to the barn, do a quick wash, and meet me near the front porch of the house. I'll go west and north."

"You gonna tell me what's happening that we've got to interrupt their work?"

"I'm getting married this morning."

"Goodness! Uh, congratulations, boss." He smiled. "Miss Reinhardt is a nice lady. You're lucky to have her. But ain't this sudden? Is everything okay?"

"It will be, presumably after the wedding."

"Okay, I'll get the boys. Anything else I can do for you?"

"Nah. Thanks for…uh…just thanks."

Jacob pushed back his hat. "Any time, boss." He hurried to a nearby stall and saddled the palomino then galloped out of the barn without a backward glance.

Nathan rotated his neck, but the tension in his shoulders still gripped his back like a steel bar. He should be happy about the wedding. Dinah was intelligent, kind, and a fellow believer. But guilt clawed him. Did Georgianna understand he had to marry again? Florence needed a mother, and if he were honest, he was lonely. The last few weeks with

Dinah had shone light into the dark places of his soul. Laughter filled the house, and even the hands seemed to be happier with her here.

Why couldn't he shake his niggling doubt?

The mantle clock chimed eleven o'clock, and Nathan's eyes shot toward the sound. How much longer before Dinah made her entrance. Pastor Youst squeezed his shoulder and winked. "You're not the first groom to be as nervous as a cat in a room full of snarling dogs. Shouldn't be much longer."

"Ready, Daddy?" Florence's voice was muted behind the bedroom door.

"Yes, honey." His heart flip-flopped. Was he ready?

The door opened, and his daughter skipped toward him, wearing her best Sunday-go-to-meeting dress, a yellow sprigged frock with a white ribbon around her waist. Her hair was plaited, and the braids wrapped around her head. She carried a basket filled with flowers. Her eyes sparkled as she grinned. "You can't see Mama Dinah, Daddy. You have to wait on the porch."

He smiled. "Is that right?"

She shrugged. "That's what Mrs. Crowell says. You and Pastor Youst go outside, then I'll throw the flowers. After that, Mama Dinah will come out." She hugged Nathan's leg and whispered, "She's pretty. You're going to like her dress."

His heart stuttered. In twenty minutes, he would be a married man. Again. To a woman he barely knew. He patted Florence's shoulder. "I can't go outside until you release me."

Florence giggled. "Sorry, Daddy."

He chuckled and followed the preacher outside. Seconds later, his daughter marched onto the porch tossing blooms to the ground. She reached her father, basket empty, and twirled in a circle. She slid her tiny hand into his, and he squeezed her fingers. He was so blessed to have this child.

Footsteps sounded, and Nathan looked toward the doorway.

Carrying a bouquet of wildflowers, Dinah wore a light-blue dress with pink pinstripes and lace collar and cuffs. Her hair had been swept up, with a few tendrils curling around her face. A wreath of flowers sat on her head. Face pale, she looked at him with uncertain eyes.

Nathan's breath caught. She was beautiful. He released Florence's hand and walked toward Dinah, his arm crooked.

She smiled, and relief flitted across her face as she slipped her hand through his elbow. Her fingers trembled, cold through his sleeve.

He laid his hand over hers and led her to the pastor. The farmhands stood in front of the porch, hats in hand, and hair plastered down. To a person, they wore satisfied smiles and seemed happy for him. They were a good group of men, and he was blessed to have them working for him.

Pastor Youst held up his hands. "We're gathered today to witness the marriage of Dinah Lucille Reinhardt and Nathan James Childs.

Marriage is given to us by God, and as such, should be part of every couple's relationship. He has deemed different responsibilities to each party. Women should obey their husbands, looking to them for leadership and guidance. Men should love their wives as Christ loved the Church." His gaze rested on Nathan. "Christ showed his love by laying down his life, and that same attitude should be held by husbands. Yes, men are head of the household, but more importantly, they must be willing to give their lives for their families. To sacrifice everything for them."

Nathan swallowed and glanced at Dinah, her lips slightly parted as she seemed to concentrate on the words. She'd shown her willingness to listen to him and follow his lead, but would she ever love him as a woman loves her husband? She'd come West to get out of a difficult situation. Would their marriage simply be a business relationship? He'd told her he'd wait until she was ready to consummate their relationship, but she might never be ready. Disappointment hollowed his chest.

He straightened his spine. She'd mentioned courting, and that's what he would do. He'd woo her, so that she would grow to love him. So she wouldn't simply marry him as a solution to her problems or for Florence's sake.

Moments later, the ceremony was over, and the men crowded onto the porch to offer congratulations.

Mrs. Crowell clanged the wrought-iron triangle that hung on the post. "I know you boys have work to do, and you might think the day is wasting, but it's lunchtime. I've rustled up some simple fare for you, and

Shorty's going to play some tunes on his harmonica so the new Mr. and Mrs. can have a dance."

Nathan's face heated. "I don't dance too well, Dinah. You might wish you were wearing boots."

"Baltimore ballrooms have made me quite adept at avoiding being trod on."

He snickered and bent in an exaggerated bow. She curtsied, then he gathered her in his arms. Shorty's harmonica wailed as Nathan waltzed her around the porch. Florence clapped her hands and giggled. "It's about time you married Mama Dinah, Daddy. You two love each other very much. Mrs. Crowell said so."

The men roared with laughter.

Nathan's face flamed, and he gaped at his daughter, then looked at Dinah, whose face was pink to the roots of her hair. Awkward silence crackled between them until she shrugged. "Children say the most outrageous things."

"Florence most of all." He huffed out a loud breath. "Thank you for going through with the wedding, Dinah. I'll do my best to make you happy."

Now, if he could only figure out how to do that.

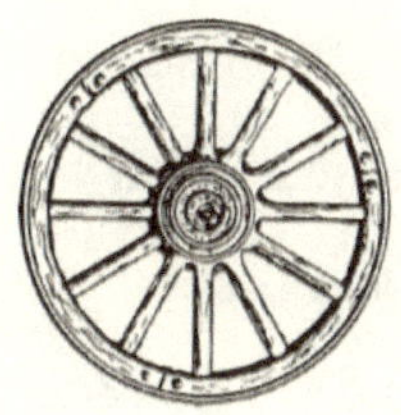

Chapter Seventeen

Dinah plucked a plump red tomato from the vine and laid it onto the growing pile in the basket. Not everyone on the prairie ate tomatoes, but she'd learned to love the tangy, luscious vegetables in Baltimore. The plants had survived the hailstorm with slight damage, so there were plenty of the juicy orbs ready for canning.

She'd helped Mother each year with their preservation but never performed the task on her own. Fortunately, Mrs. Crowell offered to help. The woman was a godsend. From preparing Dinah for the wedding five days ago to knowing the most efficient way to complete the many tasks that kept a household running, there seemed to be no end to her many talents. Would Dinah ever be as knowledgeable?

The sun warmed her back as she squatted among the plants. Another blistering day in Nebraska. Shouts from the men wafted across the hot breeze. Nathan announced at breakfast that the men would begin harvesting the wheat today. How did they stand to do such hard work in the high temperatures?

Her blouse stuck to her skin, and she pulled the material away from her neck. She removed her bonnet and fanned her face, but the motion did little to cool her. She climbed to her feet and stumbled to the pump. Dunking her head underneath, she worked the handle until water doused her with a gurgle. Sweet relief.

She ceased pumping and went inside the house for several pitchers then returned to the water station and filled the vessels to the rim. She put them on the cart with some cups and pushed the wagon toward the workers.

"Thirsty, Shorty?"

His red face streamed sweat, and his sodden hair as stuck to his scalp. "Mrs. Childs, what a wonderful surprise. I could use a drink, for sure."

She filled one of the cups, and he drank deeply before wiping his mouth on his sleeve. He set the cup on the cart and thanked her as he turned back to his work. Her chest swelled. She might not be able to harvest with the men, but she could help them bring in the crops in other ways.

Thirty minutes later, she was out of water, and the men's thirst was slaked. When she arrived at his side, Nathan had beamed at her like she was a baby who'd taken her first steps Her heart skipped a beat. He'd been solicitous and kind since the wedding, going out of his way to make things easier for her in the house. He helped with chores even after a long day in the fields or working with the animals.

Collecting the pitchers and cups, she carried them inside and dumped them in the sink. Florence sat at the table drawing a picture, and Mrs. Crowell stood in front of a cauldron of boiling water. Empty jars stood on the counter, "Good timing, Dinah. We're ready for the tomatoes."

"Perfect. I took water to the men. The heat is beastly."

"You're adjusting to life on the prairie, Dinah."

Dinah trotted outside and hefted the bushel into her arms. She lugged it into the house and set the basket on the floor near the stove. With a towel, she rubbed stray dirt off the tomatoes and handed them to the housekeeper who cut out the core then scored the skin top to bottom. With a fluid motion, she dunked the vegetable into the steaming water. Working in tandem, they performed the labor-intensive chore.

Mrs. Crowell mopped the perspiration from her face with her sleeve. "You're doing a great job, Dinah. You don't need my assistance, just more confidence."

"I'm trying to learn it all."

"Running a home on the prairie is only slightly different than in the city. In Baltimore, you would have preserved your food, washed, and mended your clothes, and any number of similar chores."

"You're right, except the volume here is so much greater. The amount of food, especially. Feeding all those men. I don't know how Cookie does it."

"He's been cooking most of his life. He was a wrangler in his early days, but then he broke his leg in a fall, and the bone healed crooked. He wasn't able to ride after that, so he stayed to rustle up the victuals." She glanced at Florence. "Another few years, and we can start training the master's daughter how to do this. She's too little yet, but by the time she's six or seven, she can do the basic steps."

Florence looked up, a frown creasing her forehead. "I'm not too little."

Dinah giggled. "Yes, you are, but you have a big heart." She wagged her index finger. "Don't be in a hurry to grow up, young lady. There's time enough for that."

"Okaaaay." She rolled her eyes and held up her paper. "I made a picture for you and Daddy. Do you like it?

The figures on the paper were misshapen with bulbous bodies and stick limbs, but there was no doubt the trio was Nathan, Dinah, and Florence. The child had even drawn her father's beard and mustache.

"You've done a wonderful job. We should put your art on the fireplace mantel so your daddy can see it. He'll love it, too."

A satisfied smiled hovering on her lips, Florence laid down the paper. "I love you, Mama Dinah."

Dinah's heart swelled. "I love you too, sweetheart."

"We're going to be short some jars, Dinah. Can you run down to the root cellar and bring up some more?"

"Absolutely. Stay put, Florence. I'll be right back." She trotted out the front door and circled the house. She lifted the door to the root cellar under the house. The stairs were rickety, and she picked her way down the treads. The coolness of the underground enclosure raised goose bumps on her arms. She crossed the dirt floor to shelves in the far corner. Empty jars stood on the top shelf, and she raised up to reach them. No good.

Squinting in the dim light, she spied a footstool tucked in the corner. Excellent. Just enough height to allow her to grab the vessels. She needed to hurry or Mrs. Crowell's work would go to waste. She dragged the short ladder to the shelf and climbed on the top rung. The rickety steps teetered under her weight. Extending her arms, she stood on her tiptoes and grabbed one of the bottles.

"Do you need help?"

Dinah whirled at the voice and lost her balance. Her arms pinwheeled as she tried to regain her equilibrium. The jar shot from her hand and landed with a crash. Her foot slipped off the platform, and she tumbled toward the ground.

Nathan raced forward, arms outstretched.

She landed in his embrace, her breath ragged.

He continued to stand with his arms around her, his chest warm and firm against her. "Are you okay? I didn't mean to startle you."

Heart thrumming in her ears, she gaped at him. Where had he come from? Why was he here?

"Dinah?" Worry creased his forehead. "Say something. Are you hurt?"

She blinked. "No. I'm fine."

He stared into her eyes, then his gaze traveled to her mouth.

Her pulse sped up, and she licked her lips. Would he kiss her? Did she want him to?

Time froze, then he lowered his face, his arms tightening. He pressed his mouth on hers, gently, tentatively.

A moan escaped, and she kissed him in return, her arms snaking around his neck as she clung to him. He might never love her as she did him, but she would show him how much she cared in this one brief moment.

"Daddy?" Florence's voice sounded outside the cellar

Nathan released Dinah as if burned. "Ah, I'm—"

Her arms dropped to her sides, and she shook her head. "Hush. Don't say anything you'll regret. You wanted a marriage in name only, and I won't jeopardize that." She turned away so he wouldn't see her heart shatter.

Chapter Eighteen

Nathan's stomach hardened. Did Dinah believe he wanted a marriage in name only? He'd made the offer at the wedding so she wouldn't feel pressured or uncomfortable at the sudden need to marry. A chill swept over him. Or did she want to keep their relationship platonic in perpetuity and used his offer as a way to do so? Hadn't she begun to care for him? Even a little? She seemed to respond to his kiss. Over the last few days, her eyes softened when she looked at him, and sometimes he'd catch her staring at him. She rarely wore the hunted expression anymore. Didn't she feel the tingles and jolts when their hands touched or their bodies were close?

He risked a glance at her. She'd already turned away and busied herself with the jars as if their conversation—and kiss—meant nothing. He blew out a deep breath, raking his fingers through his hair. His lips still held the memory of her mouth, warm and pliable. She'd seemed lost in their embrace then Florence's interruption came, and Dinah's eyes had shuttered, and she rejected him.

Stung, he frowned. She'd burrowed her way into his heart, bit by bit. First, with the love and attention she'd shown to Florence. Then she'd been tenacious in her efforts to learn the ways of the prairie and how to run his household. Her stalwart but quiet faith and childlike joy at each new discovery of life on the plains made him smile. In fact, he'd smiled a lot since she'd come. The grief that he wore like a cloak was slipping off his shoulders.

A harsh laugh escaped. Her rebuff after his many dismissive thoughts was nothing less than he deserved, but pain knifed his heart nonetheless.

"Daddy?"

He moved to the doorway. "In here, Florence. I'll be out in a moment. Please stay put."

"Okay." Disappointment seemed to color her voice.

Or was he transferring his letdown to his daughter? He shook his head and pivoted toward Dinah. "Please let me help with the jars."

"As you wish." She stepped back from the shelves. "But I don't want to keep you from your tasks. Why did you come down?"

"To let you know I need to go into town for supplies. We've run out of fencing as well as some other items. I wondered if you'd like to join me. The journey would give you an opportunity to get off the farm for a bit, browse in the mercantile, or visit Livvy."

Her eyes lit, then dimmed, and she shook her head. "Mrs. Crowell wouldn't appreciate me abandoning her to finish the canning, so I'll have to pass."

"I understand, although she's handled the task alone in the past."

Dinah shrugged. "True, but to leave would also set a bad example for Florence. She needs to see the importance of keeping a commitment, no matter how inconvenient or disappointing."

"Of course. I should have thought of the influence on Florence." His face heated as he handed her several jars. "If you create a list, I can do your shopping."

"It's only been a week since our last trip. I don't need anything, but thank you for asking." She tucked the jars into a basket on the floor. "On second thought, perhaps a peppermint stick or other sweet treat for Florence."

Nathan pulled down six more glass containers. "A wonderful idea." He gestured to the collection of jars. "Will this be enough?"

"I think so." Her smile didn't reach her eyes. "Thanks for helping." She turned and climbed the stairs, her shoulders slumped.

He followed her and blinked against the harsh sunlight.

"Daddy! You and Mama Dinah took forever. I waited a very long time." Florence skipped beside him as he made his way into the house.

"Patience is a virtue, honey."

Her brow creased. "What's a virtue?"

"Uh…"

"Being a good girl." Dinah set the jars on the counter then tapped her finger on Florence's nose. "And patience means you wait even when you don't want to. Now, your daddy needs to go to town, and we have work to do here, so you will learn about patience. Isn't that exciting?"

Florence looked skeptical, and Nathan pressed his lips to keep from chuckling. He bowed. "Ladies, is there anything else I can do before I bid you adieu."

Mrs. Crowell waved her wooden spoon at the dirt he'd tracked into the kitchen. "Clean up after yourself."

"I can do that, Mrs. Crowell." Dinah moved to the sink. "He needs to get on the road."

"Then what sort example would I be for Florence?"

She flushed and marched to the basket of tomatoes, her back stiff. "Good point. Thank you for the reminder."

"Dinah…never mind." He grabbed the broom and swept up the nuggets of dirt that had fallen off his boots. "Don't hold dinner. I don't know how long I'll be." He fled the kitchen and hurried to the barn where he wouldn't have to worry about saying the wrong thing or hurting someone's feelings.

In quick order, he hitched the horse to the buckboard and leapt onto the seat. He tapped the horse's rump with the reins, and the wagon lurched forward. Very little dust rose from the ground because of the recent rainstorm, so he left his handkerchief wrapped around his neck. The sun warmed his back, and birds swooped overhead. Creaks from the wheels and squeaks from the leather harness created an off-key melody.

Content to let the horse take lead, Nathan slouched forward, arms on his knees, the traces held loosely between his fingers. He gazed at the stubbled wheat field, its exposed dirt fragrant and musky on the wind. Another day or two, and he'd plant soybeans. Grateful for the additional income the beans provided, he'd learned the trick of double cropping the land shortly after arriving.

A prairie chicken darted across the lane about thirty yards ahead, her warbling cry reminiscent of laughter. The memory surfaced of the day he'd seen the birds with Dinah. She'd been awed then tickled with the awkward fowl. Her wide-eyed acceptance of his tales and explanation fed his pride.

He blew out a loud breath. "I sure messed up today. Dinah has every right to be upset with me. I should never have kissed her without asking first."

The horse's ears flattened, and he bobbed his head as if he were agreeing with Nathan's soliloquy.

"Thanks, Cinnamon. I don't need your two cents." Nathan rubbed his face. "One minute I promise myself I'm going to woo Dinah, and the next I'm kissing her as if we were wed…well, for real. What am I going to do to fix this situation?"

Love her, My son.

"Got any specifics, God?"

Silence.

Nathan chuckled. He already knew the answer. Paul outlined how love should be handled in one of his letters to the Corinthians: with patience and kindness, not being proud or selfish.

"Okay, God, You know I can be abrupt, hardheaded, and stubborn, so I'm going to need your help to change my behavior. Help us figure out this marriage thing. We're married, and that's not going to change. I'd like to have a real marriage with Dinah. I love her." He blinked. He cared for her. A lot. But love? His heart tripped. Yeah, he loved her, and he'd do whatever it took to get his bride to feel the same way about him.

And we know that all things work together for good to them that love God, to them who are called according to His purpose.

"You sent Dinah to me, didn't you, Lord. For me to protect and provide for this sweet woman. And to heal my broken heart." Tears pricked the backs of his eyes. "Thank you, Father. I will love her as You've loved me, and whatever happens is okay by me."

Chapter Nineteen

A warm breeze fluttered the living room curtains and ruffled Dinah's hair as she sat in the rocking chair by the window. The oil lamp burned steady under the glass chimney. In the distance, the rattle of wagon wheels mingled with the clip-clop of horse's hooves. She laid down the shirt she was mending and looked through the panes. The setting sun created an aura around the buckboard and the driver's form sitting high in the seat. Her pulse sped up. Nathan was home.

While he was gone, she'd had plenty of time to ruminate over what happened in the root cellar. She had overreacted and hurt a very good man. She'd prayed for forgiveness, but her heart still wasn't clean. She needed to apologize to him and had rehearsed her words multiple times. She nibbled on her lower lip. Would he be willing to make amends?

The wagon drew closer then disappeared into the barn. She glanced at the mantel clock then jumped up and rushed into the bedroom to check her appearance. Heart pounding like a schoolgirl's, she stared at her reflection in the mirror above the washstand. Errant strands of hair dangled around her face, and her bun was off kilter.

With quick motions, she undid the pins, brushed the tresses until they were smooth, then wound her hair into place. She pinched her cheeks to give them color. She sighed and ran her hands down the front of her dress to press out the wrinkles. Her appearance was as good as it would get. She straightened her spine and walked into the living room.

Footsteps clomped on the porch, then the door swung open. Nathan came inside, a canvas sack in each hand. A cautious smile curved his lips. His eyes were clouded. "How was your day? Did you and Mrs. Crowell finish the canning all right?"

Hands fisted in front of her, she nodded. "A good amount that should take us through much of the winter. There are still blooms and unripe tomatoes on the vines, so we'll have more to preserve. I hope you like tomatoes because were certainly have a bumper crop." She pressed her lips together to stop herself from rambling.

"That's good. I've learned to love them, and Mrs. Crowell has a wonderful recipe for some sort of sauce. I'm sure she'll teach you how to make it."

She gestured to his bags. "Florence will be happy. You seem to have bought out the store's supply of peppermint sticks."

He chuckled and walked to the dining room table where he laid down the pouches. "Don't peek. I picked up some household supplies that

Mrs. Garlinger said would be helpful. You didn't ask for them, but she said most wives would appreciate these items."

"Before you do that, I'd like to apologize for…earlier…the way I acted…what I said." Her chin trembled, and she hesitated. Why did she have to cry at the drop of a hat? He'd think her nothing but a ninny. "You have been nothing but kind to me, and I've returned your goodness with arguments and fractious words. I have no excuse for my behaviors, and I hope you'll forgive me."

His eyes glittered in the flickering light. Was he angry? Would he refuse to forgive her? Dinah's pulse tripped.

Nathan's face lit up. "There's nothing to forgive. The journey into town and back gave me lots of time to pray, and I've been…uh…made aware that my thoughts and behavior have been less than honorable. I'm sorry that I've upset you, and we've had times of misunderstanding. How about if we put everything behind us and start again?"

The tightness in her chest eased. "I'd like that."

He rubbed his hands together. "Excellent. And what better way to do that than to see what I've brought you." He pulled out a chair and gestured for her to sit. He sat beside her and drew the bags toward himself. "We can look at most of this tomorrow or later, but I have a special gift for tonight."

Her breath hitched, and she tried to peer into the bag where he'd stuck his hand.

"Hey, no snooping." He pulled the pouch straps together. "Close your eyes."

She grinned and did as he instructed.

He leaned close. "Are you peeking?"

His musky scent permeated her senses, and her heart thudded. "No. Now, hurry up."

Rustling, then a faint thud on the table. "Okay, you can look now."

A thick volume with a chocolate-brown cover, etched in gilt lettering, sat in front of her. She stroked the book with gentle fingers. "*The Innocents Abroad*! Oh, Nathan, I've heard about Mr. Twain's book, but I never dreamed I would own it. He traveled to many exotic locations. I can't wait to read it."

"I'm glad you like it."

"Like it? I treasure it." Her smile faltered. "Did it cost a lot? Books are a luxury, Nathan. I'm touched you spent your hard-earned money on a book."

"I promised to make you happy. This is a tiny start." He rose and held out his hand. "Now, leave the gift, and let's sit on the porch for a bit. The sunset is beautiful, and I'm sure you worked hard today." He glanced at the rocker where her abandoned mending lay. "First, canning then sewing. Do you never quit?"

She shrugged. "Do you?"

"Point taken. Well, we both deserve a break." He wiggled his fingers. "Join me."

Dinah's Dilemma

Dinah laced her fingers in his, the warmth of his palm sent shivers up her arm and down her spine. She followed him outside, and they seated themselves on the rocking chairs. Orange and purple streaks etched the velvet sky. Bats chittered and swooped. The breeze was warm and moist.

She glanced at Nathan, his profile shadowed in the dim light. She'd planned to finish her apology with a confession about her relationship to her brothers, but she'd lost her nerve after his kind words and request for forgiveness. Then there was the gift. She couldn't bear to ruin the special moment with the ugly truth.

Would there ever be a good opportunity to tell him? The month since her arrival had changed her life in ways she'd never imagined. She was learning to be adept at running a household as her skills improved, giving her confidence that she was a capable woman. That she could do more than make tea and carry on interesting conversations in a drawing room. Best of all, she was Florence's Mama Dinah. She may not have given birth to the child, but she loved the little girl as if she were her own.

Nathan might not love her, but they were getting along, developing a friendship. She sighed. Who was she fooling? She wanted to be more than friends. In the few short weeks since she'd come to Nebraska, she'd fallen in love with the beefy, broad-shouldered man. Yes, he was handsome, but his gentleness, integrity, and quiet faith were the qualities that drew her to him. If she told him about the boys, all would be lost.

A shooting star raced across the heavens. A message from God that she should seek His help? But until she untangled her web of deceit, she didn't deserve to talk to Him.

Crickets chirped, their song pulsing in the hot air. Nathan peeked at Dinah, who seemed to be having some sort of argument with herself. He smiled. She was one of the most tenacious women he'd ever met, driven in the expectations and demands she put on herself. "Thank you for coming outside. We need to take advantage of the lovely nights while we can. Summer will be gone before you know it, and we'll be shivering in the cold."

She waved her hand in front of her face. "After temperatures like today, I'm looking forward to the cool nights."

He chuckled. "And in January, you'll be complaining you can't get warm enough."

She smiled, and her teeth flashed in the moonlight. "I'll take my chances."

"Being from Maryland, I thought you'd appreciate our hot summers."

"An interesting choice of words." She crossed her arms. "My favorite season is autumn because the leaves change color, and the air becomes more crisp."

"I'd like to know more about what you like. We've not been able to spend much time alone. Breakfast, dinner, and early evening are shared with Florence, and as much as I love my curious, rambunctious child, her presence leaves little opportunity for in-depth conversation."

"What would you like to know? I've not led an exciting life."

"What's your favorite color? Your favorite author? Your favorite food?"

"Red. Jane Austen. Cake." She ticked the items on her fingers. "Now, you."

"Blue. Verne. Steak." He grinned. "Not at all compatible with you."

She shifted toward him and tucked her chin in her hand. "Okay, favorite song."

"Anything by Stephen Foster. You?"

"I love his music, so peppy."

A gust of wind wafted her scent of soap toward him, and his chest constricted. He licked his lips. "Hmm. What about when you were a child? What did you like to do?"

"Like any young girl, I had a tea set and dolls to whom I told my darkest secrets. I also liked to skip rope. Nothing unusual. How about you? I'll bet you were rough and tumble, climbing trees, and playing soldiers. Did you have a slingshot?"

"Any boy worth his salt owned a slingshot. I'll have you know I was quite good with it." He cocked his head. "But I'd like to hear more about you as a little girl. I'm imagining you all dressed up with your hair pulled back and tied with a large ribbon, a large red ribbon that set off your lovely brown hair. You arrange everything just so before sitting down in your floral dress and white pinafore."

"Of course, the table had to be set correctly." Dinah snickered. "I've not changed much in that regard."

He reached over and cradled her hand in his, her small palm nestling with his in sweet perfection. She stilled at his touch. Would she pull away? A moment later, her hand relaxed, and he released a quiet breath. He needed to maintain the light mood. "Seeing how you've acted here, I'll bet you were curious about everything."

"Except bugs." She shuddered. "I don't like bugs one bit. Crawly and creepy. You can keep them."

"I'll try to protect you, but the Nebraska prairie has plenty of insects. You can hear the crickets, but a farmer's worst fear may be grasshoppers. They can decimate a crop in short order. I pray we don't see an infestation in my lifetime, but my hope is probably unrealistic."

"I will pray, too."

"Thank you, Dinah. You're a good woman."

She sighed.

"A penny for your thoughts."

"They'll cost you more than that." Her voice was guarded, and she removed her hand from his.

Nathan frowned. Had he unearthed unpleasant memories? How badly had her father's gambling affected the family, to say nothing of the war that raged almost in her backyard? What atrocities had she experienced?

He pushed to his feet and forced a laugh. "Then we'll have to go in the house where I keep my gold. Will that be enough?"

"Perhaps." She snickered. "I'll consider your offer."

The tension melted from his back, and he pulled her to him in an embrace. He stroked her jaw with his thumb and pressed a kiss to her forehead, then on the tip of her nose, and finally on her lips.

An emotion he couldn't read played across her face in the light coming through the window. She blinked then fumbled for the doorknob. "I'm suddenly quite tired, Nathan. I'd like to retire."

"Of course." He shoved his hands into his pockets and stepped back.

She slipped inside and closed the door, the lock sliding closed with a *snick.*

He walked off the porch and tromped toward the barn. Had he offended her? Saddened her? Frightened her? They'd mended their fences with the apologies, and their conversation had gone well. She'd held his hand, seeming happy to do so. He thought she might welcome the chaste kisses, but his gesture was apparently too soon. She'd skedaddled into the bedroom.

Wooing Georgianna hadn't been this hard. No matter. Getting Dinah to care for him might not be an easy task, but gaining her love would be worth the effort.

Dinah's Dilemma

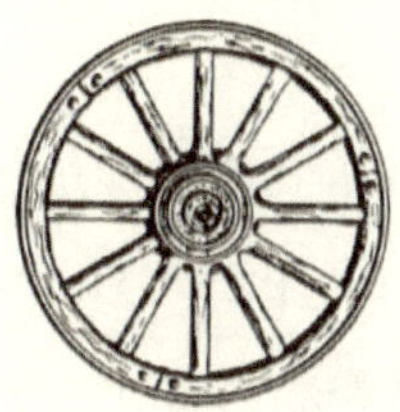

Chapter Twenty

The day promised to be another scorcher. Barely above the horizon, the sun's ray glistened on the dew as Nathan led Cinnamon out of the barn. Harnessed to the cart, the horse nickered. "I agree, Cinnamon. Too hot a day to work, but the fences won't mend themselves. I promise you a nice rubdown tonight and an extra rasher of oats. How does that sound?"

Another nicker, and Nathan grinned. "Then let's get started." They sauntered toward the lone figure about three hundred yards away. In the distance, Jacob waved then squatted on the ground. The ever-present breeze tugged at Nathan's hat and ruffled Cinnamon's mane. As they arrived at his foreman's location, Nathan raised an eyebrow. Dark clouds scudded across the gray sky that moments before had been clear and blue. "Not sure how much we'll get done before the storm hits. Kind of unexpected."

Jacob nodded. "Hopefully, it will be a quick shower and cool us down, although the new soybeans could use a bit a rain."

"Been an unusual summer, Jacob."

The older man cocked his head. "You talkin' about the weather or the new missus?"

"Both, but mostly Dinah. Nothing much gets past you, does it?"

"Not with the number of years I've got under my belt, son. I was married twenty-five years and been widowed almost as many, but I still remember what having a wife was like. And you're a man who looks like he's got a lot on his mind. Ain't been but a week since the wedding. You two are still trying to figure out how to be married."

Nathan handed him a hammer. "You can say that again. Seems we take two steps forward and three steps back. Kind of cliché, but I feel like I'm walking on eggshells sometimes. She had a rough go of it when she was growing up, so she's struggling with trusting me. I've let her down a couple of times, and we've argued."

"Sounds like a marriage to me." He chuckled. "Listen, son, marriage takes work. A lot of work even when both parties love each other and have known each other before the big day. Two people come to the relationship carrying their hurts and fears and bad experiences, and those things impact every word and deed. 'Tis easy to misunderstand the other person and take offense." He gestured to the broken fence with his tool. "Just like this fence that needs constant maintenance, a marriage needs to be kept in good condition. You gotta say what you're thinkin' and feelin', otherwise, the rot can infiltrate, and the next thing you know, you're driftin' apart."

150

"But how can we drift apart before we even know each other?" Nathan pushed his Stetson back on his head. "I'm making efforts to get to know her. We had a good conversation last night."

"But?"

Nathan's face heated. "Uh, well, we agreed to keep the marriage in name only until she was ready, but I ruined the mood when I kissed her good night. She asked me to leave then went into the house."

"What did she say *exactly*?"

"She said she was suddenly quite tired and wanted to retire."

Jacob guffawed and clapped Nathan on the back. "Sounds like she needed time to think over what happened. You set her back on her heels, and she wasn't sure how to react, so she fled." He grinned. "I think her reaction is a good sign, son. Just give her time. Continue to court her and treat her as the special gal she is. She'll come around."

"You think so?"

"Yep." He wagged his finger at Nathan. "I know you're a prayin' man, but you gotta be sure to cover this situation in prayer. God will see you two through."

Nathan's chest lightened. "Thanks, Jacob. I—"

Hoofbeats thundered, and he whirled toward the sound.

Bent over his horse's neck, Sheriff Denard raced toward them. The animal's ears were laid back, its sides heaving. Foam gathered at the horse's mouth. Under his Stetson, Alfred's face was red, his mouth set in a slash. Sweat streamed down his cheeks.

Whatever his friend came to say, it would not be good news. Of that, he was sure. Nathan narrowed his eyes and exchanged glances with Jacob. A shudder slithered up his spine. Had something terrible happened in town? To Livvy? "What do you suppose has him in such an all-fired-up hurry?"

Jacob shrugged. "Guess we're about to find out."

Alfred pulled up on the reins, and the horse's front feet came off the ground as he danced to a stop. The sheriff leapt from the saddle and wrapped the traces around the fence rail. "Nathan, I'm glad I found you." He glanced at Jacob. "I've got news."

Jacob touched two fingers to the brim of his hat and bent to retrieve his hammer. "I got work to do." He grabbed Cinnamon's bridle and sauntered off.

When his foreman was about fifty yards away, Nathan lifted his eyes to Alfred, winded as if he, and not the horse, had run the distance. "Livvy? Did something happen?"

The sheriff shook his head, then pulled out a handkerchief, removed his hat, and wiped the perspiration from his face. He shoved the linen into his pocket and swallowed. "I heard back from my connection in Maryland. A rather lengthy telegram."

"Your contact has money."

"Yes, which is why he is often able to ferret out information more, shall we say, traditional methods fail to garner."

Nathan's heart pounded. Maryland. This was about Dinah. He frowned. "Well, what did he find out?"

"Steady yourself, my friend. Dinah has been withholding her family relations." Alfred gripped his shoulder. "She's the daughter of her mother's first marriage to Uwe Reinhardt. Her father died when she was fairly young, and her mother remarried Chester Simpkins. He's the one with the gambling problems. They have two sons, Jerome and Herbert."

Waves of nausea rocked Nathan. His vision swirled, and he swayed on his feet. "Simpkins? Of the Bloody Tubs? Who murdered my wife?" His hands fisted, and he twisted away from Alfred's hold.

"The very same." Alfred rubbed his jaw. "I take it from the stunned look on your face this is new information to you."

Nathan swiped at his eyes. "She's said nothing about her brothers." His eyes widened. "The gang doesn't allow women to join, but surely she knows about her siblings' despicable activities." Memories of Dinah's guilt-ridden face paraded through his mind. He sagged against the fence and huffed out a breath. "She knows."

"There's more. The boys were captured in a tiny outpost called Bethesda. Not much but a church, school, blacksmith's shop, and post office, where it just so happens the boys' likenesses were spied on their wanted posters. They should have headed for one of the larger cities to blend in, but I guess they're not too smart. They're sitting in a Baltimore jail waiting for trial."

Breath ragged and loud in his ears, Nathan whipped his face toward Alfred. "Will I be called to testify? Should I travel to Maryland?" A chill swept over him. "Do I tell her what I've learned? What if she chooses to remain silent? How can I trust her?"

"Only you can determine those answers, but I'd pray long and hard before taking action. What's done can't be undone."

Nathan rubbed the back of his neck. *Dear God, how could You let this happen?*

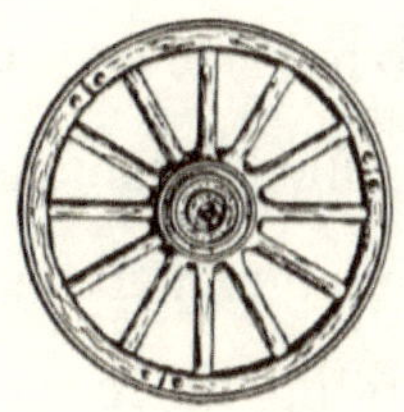

Chapter Twenty-One

Cloth in hand, Dinah lifted the iron from the fire and pressed the wrinkles from Florence's skirt. She smiled as each crease disappeared under the hot tool. A tedious chore, but rewarding. Perspiration lined her face. She glanced at Mrs. Crowell who stood at the sink and washed dishes. "Where is Nathan today?"

"I think he's mending fences. Do you need something?"

"No." She set the iron back on the rack over the fire and hung the skirt over the back of one of the dining room chairs. Grabbing a towel, she blotted the sweat from her skin. "We…uh…need to discuss something, and I'd hoped to do so at breakfast, but he failed to appear."

"Must have wanted an early start of since the sky promises a storm later." Mrs. Crowell dried her hands then leaned on the counter. "I don't want to overstep, but you seem upset. I've a good ear if you'd like to talk."

Should she tell the housekeeper her sordid story? Would the woman judge her, finding her deceit deplorable and unforgiveable as Nathan would if he knew? She dragged out a chair and flopped into the seat. Elbows on the table, she dropped her head into her hands. Tears seeped from her eyes then streamed in a steady flow.

Mrs. Crowell rushed to her side and sat. She wrapped an arm around Dinah's shoulder and pulled her into a warm embrace. "I knew something was wrong, child. You let it all out, and then we'll talk."

Dinah wept, her cries filling the room as she released the pent up fear and sadness. Years of bottling up the shame and embarrassment of her family's actions, frustration at a society who looked down their nose on a family in need rather than provide assistance, and fear of being caught in the web of lies she'd created. Her nose clogged, and she pulled a handkerchief from her pocket.

Her sobs subsided, and she wiped her eyes. "I don't know where to start."

"How about at the beginning?" Mrs. Crowell tucked an errant strand of hair behind Dinah's ear then patted her arm. "There's no problem too big for our heavenly Father. If you'd rather not tell me, you can take your problem to Him."

"I don't think God wants to hear from me." Her lip trembled. "We've not spoken in a while, and I've done so many bad things, He's surely turned His back on me."

"Nonsense. Christ pardoned the thief on the cross. He will do the same for you."

Dinah looked at Mrs. Crowell with a shuddering breath. Expecting to find reproach and condemnation, she was stunned to see nothing but love and acceptance on the housekeeper's face. More tears threatened, but she blinked them away. With a nod, she sat up and began to share everything that had happened from her father's gambling problems and subsequent fall from grace to her brothers' connection with the murderous gang and their part in the death of Georgianna.

"Nathan will never forgive me when he discovers my identity, and he'll send me away. I've been so afraid to tell him. He's been hurting for a long time. And now I love Florence." She frowned. "What a mess I've created."

"And you love Mr. Childs, too."

"Yes." Dinah's voice was barely a whisper.

"You need to tell him, child. You can't begin your marriage on a series of falsehoods. Nathan is a good man, and he loves you. I've seen how he looks at you. He may be angry at first, but he'll come to his senses, and your relationship will be stronger."

"Will you pray for me? For us?"

Mrs. Crowell cradled Dinah's hands. "Dear heavenly Father, Dinah is coming to you with a broken and contrite heart. She realizes the error of her ways and wishes to be cleansed of the lies and deceit that have become part of her life. She's afraid about the future and afraid to talk to Nathan. Please give her Your peace and wrap both of these precious young people in Your arms. Give them strength to face this difficulty. Bless them as only You can. We pray these things in the name of Your Son, Jesus. Amen."

Dinah lifted her head and smiled. The tension that had gripped every muscle in her body was gone, her spirit light. In an instant, God had removed the darkness and filled her with peace. "Thank you, Mrs. Crowell. My problems still exist, but God has taken my burdens on Himself. Whatever happens, I know is for my best, even if I suffer pain and hurt. After all, there are consequences to my actions."

"My brave girl." Mrs. Crowell rose. "Do you want to find Nathan?"

"No, I don't want to interrupt his day. I will tell him when he comes back to the house, but until then I'll focus on my chores."

"All right. Then before you take up the ironing again, would you mind going to the barn and asking one of the hands to bring in the wash tub and fill it? I'd like to do the curtains today."

"Yes, ma'am." She went to the bedroom, poured water from the ewer into the bowl, and rinsed her swollen face. She pulled out her disheveled bun then brushed her hair and pinned it into place. With a spring in her step, she left the house and headed to the barn. It would be difficult to share the truth with Nathan, but she looked forward to the time in a few short hours when there would be no more secrets between them.

She entered the cavernous barn. Voices at the far end stopped her. Her gaze swept the building. Whomever was speaking must be in one of the stalls. Should she alert them to her presence?

"I appreciate you taking time to come out personally. You could have sent your deputy with the information." Nathan's voice was muffled.

Dinah's heart skittered. Was God giving her the opportunity to speak with Nathan now? But who was he with? She'd wait until whoever it was departed.

"You and I have been friends for too long. I wouldn't let you hear this kind of thing from anyone but me. I've got to head back into town, but you send one of your boys if you need me." Sheriff Denard's voice filtered toward her, and her stomach tightened.

"Yeah. I still don't know what to do. How could she do this?"

"You need to hear her side of the story, Nathan. Until you walk in her shoes you can't understand what's she gone through. And you need to pray about the situation, like I said. Don't do this on your own."

"How can I love her and hate her at the same time?"

Horse hooves clattered, and Dinah couldn't hear the sheriff's response, but Nathan's words knifed her heart. Footsteps then Sheriff Denard led his black gelding from the stall, mounted the animal, and rode out the far end of the building.

Dinah pressed her hands against her chest and rushed forward before she lost her nerve. As she reached the entrance to the stall, she came face-to-face with Nathan, his face a mixture of confusion, anger, and disgust. Her eyes widened, and her tongue cleaved to the roof of her mouth. "Nathan." Her voice squeaked, and she cleared her throat. "Nathan, we need to talk. There's something I need to tell you."

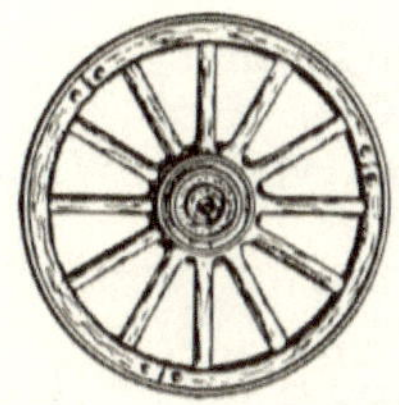

Chapter Twenty-Two

Nathan crossed his arms and gritted his teeth. He needed time to process the information Alfred had sprung on him, yet Dinah stood before him. Face etched in worry, she wrung her hands and shuffled her feet in the dirt floor. He didn't want to handle this yet. He wanted to swing the hammer until his shoulders ached, pounding away his frustration, anger, and disappointment with every strike on the posts.

"Now isn't a good time, Dinah. I've got work to do, and uh…things to think about. Please go back to the house. We'll discuss whatever you need tonight, after dinner."

She shook her head. Tears brimmed in her eyes, and she blinked them away. "This conversation won't wait, Nathan. We need to talk now."

"Fine." He set his jaw. "I'm listening."

"Is there somewhere we could sit?" Her gaze ricocheted around the barn. "You might be more comfortable."

"The barn is for working, not for sitting. There's nothing here."

Her face paled, and she nodded. "Okay." She licked her lips.

His gaze shot to her mouth, the memory of their kisses sweeping through his mind. He blew out a breath. Focus, man!

Dinah paced for a moment then stopped in front of him. "I've withheld information from you, Nathan. What I'm about to say will be painful, and I'm sorry. It was not my intention to hurt you." She blew out a shaky breath. "My given name is Dinah Reinhardt as I'd told you, but my mother remarried after my father's death to a man named Chester Simpkins. They had two boys who are quite a bit younger than me: Jerome and Herbert. They belong to—"

"The Bloody Tubs." He couldn't listen to the anguish in her voice any longer and raked his fingers through his hair. "And I know about the hand they had in my wife's death."

She gaped at him, her eyes wide and fearful. "How long—"

"Since a few moments ago. Alfred was here and told me."

"But how did he find out?"

"Shortly after you arrived, I tasked him with digging into your background. After years of being a Pinkerton agent, I recognize when someone is lying, or at least not being completely honest. I sensed you were hiding something and asked him to check into your background."

Her shoulders slumped, and silent tears tumbled down her cheeks.

Nathan's heart clenched at her obvious sorrow, and he wrapped his arms around his waist. He could not let her emotions influence him. Justice had to be served even if it meant losing the woman he loved.

Because, he did love her. With his whole being. He narrowed his eyes. "Did you know when we met that your brothers killed Georgianna?"

"No!" Her voice cracked. "I didn't find out about them until the night you gave me their names."

"Then why didn't you tell me of your relationship?"

She began to pace again. "I don't know. I was afraid. Afraid that you wouldn't believe that I had nothing to do with their nefarious activities. Ever. And afraid you'd send me away."

He yanked off his hat and rubbed his throbbing forehead. "Did you hear what Alfred said? Is that why you decided to tell me about them yourself? Hoping if I hear about them from your lips, I'd somehow be more forgiving."

"I didn't know about Alfred." She waved her hand toward the house. "Mrs. Crowell will tell you that we talked…and prayed about the situation. I got up this morning with the conviction I needed to tell you…everything, but then you didn't come inside for breakfast. Anyway, afterward, she sent me out here to get one of the boys to fill the washtub for her. When I heard your voice, I thought God was providing the chance to tell you…to make things right." She bowed her head. "You have no reason to believe me, but what I'm telling you is the truth."

"You're right, I shouldn't believe you, and I'm not sure that I do." He stuffed his hands in his pockets and turned away. "And I'm not sure I want to be married to a woman who would keep such a terrible secret from me. How do I know you aren't withholding other information? What sort of example are you setting for my daughter?"

"I—"

Screaming sounded from the house, and his head whipped toward the noise. He raced toward the door, Dinah on his heels.

Mrs. Crowell stood on the porch waving her arms over her head, a sheet of paper clutched in one hand. "Mr. Childs, come quickly. It's Florence. She's gone."

His stomach fell, and he stumbled. His precious baby girl was missing. Where could she be? He ran up the stairs and grabbed his housekeeper by the shoulders. "Tell me everything. When is the last time you saw her?"

With trembling fingers, she gave him the note. "This was on her pillow. I laid her down for a nap after Dinah came out here, thinking to keep the child out from underfoot while we worked." She gulped. "I heard a noise and was afraid she'd fallen out of bed, so I went up to check on her. The sheets were rumpled, and the quilt is missing, and so is our little girl." She put her hands over her face and sobbed.

Nathan raked his eyes over the page: I HAV YUR KID. PUT 5000 DOLLURS IN A BAG AND COME TO THE GRAVEYARD OUTSIDE OF TOWN AT MIDNITE. NO LAWMEN OR SHE DIES. BAD CHOICE TO MARY THAT SIMPKINS GURL

"Oh, Nathan." Beside him, Dinah stared at the paper in his hand. "This is all my fault."

"What did you do?" He crumpled the note and hurled it on the ground.

Her gaze shifted to the missive, and she rubbed her arms as if chilled. "Nothing more than what you know. But there was a man who came looking for a job. Jacob turned him away. As the man was leaving, he saw me. He's from Maryland and the reason I fled. One day, I was with friends getting on the streetcar, and he attacked me…kicking and punching…yelling he would hurt me like Jerome and Herbert hurt his brother. Fortunately, the crowd stopped him, but I realized I'd never be free of my brothers unless I moved far away. That very day, I met Mrs. Crenshaw, and she sent me to you." She swiped at a tear. "The man took Florence to hurt me. I'm so sorry."

His lips curled into a sneer. "This conversation isn't over, but the first priority is to rescue my daughter." He pointed at her with his index finger. "And you better pray she's alive when we find her."

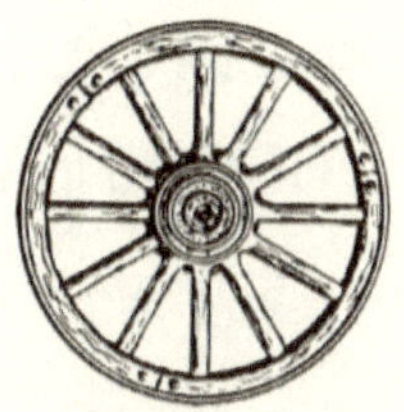

Chapter Twenty-Three

Nathan turned away from Dinah's tear-streaked face. If he caved in to acknowledge the agony of her distress, he'd lose focus, and he couldn't afford to make mistakes. Not when his daughter's life depended on his ability to find her. But the desire to draw Dinah into his arms, stroke her silky hair, and whisper that everything would be all right threatened to overwhelm him.

He straightened his spine. A Pinkerton did not let personal feelings get in the way of a job. And that's how he needed to approach this nightmare, because if he thought about Florence's terror at being abducted by a strange man and subjected to...

"Cinnamon." He strode into the stall where the beautiful stallion waited. With practiced motions, Nathan saddled the giant horse in record time. "Dear God, don't let anything happen to my little girl. I don't know what I'll do if I lose her, too."

"Nathan, I want to come to...to help." Dinah's small voice sounded from behind.

He whirled and grimaced. "Don't you think you've *helped* enough already?"

She jerked back as if he'd slapped her, her face draining of color. "No, I don't. This is my fault, so I should look for her."

"Sounds like all you want to do is ease your guilty conscience." He tried not to wince at the acid that colored his words. "You'll be an impediment. I can't worry about your safety and Florence's. Stay here and pray."

"But—"

"Nathan!" Alfred galloped into the barn, his mount lathered. "Jacob caught up with me. Told me about Florence. I'll go back into town and pull together a posse, but I need a fresh horse. I've worn out this poor beast."

"I was just about to head out. I can't wait for you."

Alfred jumped off the horse and grabbed his arm. "Don't go off half cocked. We need to be organized about looking for this guy. You know that from your Pinkerton days. Don't go it alone. You'll get hurt…or worse."

"Sheriff." Dinah reached out. "Sheriff, I'd like to join the search party."

His gaze raked her up and down, then his piercing eyes rested on her face. "Can you handle a gun? Ride a horse as if your life depended on it? Keep your wits about you?"

"Yes to all your questions. I'll do whatever you say." She swiped at the moisture on her cheeks, determination in her stiff posture.

"Fine—"

"Alfred." Nathan frowned.

Alfred slashed the air with his hand. "We need every able-bodied person to make this plan work. I know you're angry and scared right now, but don't add stupid to the mix. Now, saddle up. Mind if I take Cinnamon since he's ready to ride?

"He's yours."

"Great. You two grab the farmhands and start tracking this guy. Be sure to leave clues for us to follow. I'll be back with more help as soon as I can." He climbed onto the stallion and galloped out of the barn.

Nathan nodded at his retreating form and swallowed against the lump in this throat. His baby girl was in the hands of a desperate man. He fisted his hands and punched the wall. Pain shot up his arm, and his knuckles bled. He'd been told to come alone, but he couldn't rescue his daughter and ensure this creep came to justice. Without the posse, he'd be tempted to shoot the man and dispense his own justice.

Dinah rushed toward him. "Nathan."

He held up his uninjured hand. "Don't come near me." He yanked his handkerchief from his pocket and tied it around his throbbing hand. Not the smartest move he'd ever made, but he needed to do something with his frustration. "First, run into the house, and tell Mrs. Crowell to pack up some food. Might have to be gone a couple of days." He stiffened and shook his head. "Ring the bell while you're there. That will call the hands, and we can tell them what's going on. Then come back and help me saddle any remaining horses. Think you can handle that?"

"Yes." Clouded and dark, her eyes darted from his face to the ground. She nodded, lifted her skirts, and ran out of the barn.

"Dear God, please keep Florence safe. Tell her I'm coming for her." He scrubbed at his face with ice-cold fingers then blew out a deep breath. "And keep me from killing this guy, if possible. It's not my job to judge, but I'd sure like to hurt him like he's hurt me."

One of the horses whinnied, and Nathan hurried to the stall and began to harness the palomino. With every move he made, his broken skin protested. Spots of blood dotted the handkerchief. He could imagine Alfred's smirk when he saw his wound.

His shoulders tight, Nathan finished with the horse and moved to the next stall. Time blurred as he saddled each mount. The farmhands began to show up, thundering into the barn on horseback and foot. A cacophony of voices filled the barn as they rushed to him, plying him with questions.

He held up his hand. "I'll outline the plan after everyone is here. Meanwhile, fill your canteens and grab your bedrolls from the bunkhouse then report back here."

The men hurried from the building, their voices fading.

Dinah returned with a basket full of towel-wrapped packages, her face flushed and blotchy. She'd also slung several canteens over her shoulder. They bumped her hips and side as she ran toward him.

Nathan flared his nostrils. How could she look so beautiful in such a disheveled state? Why would he notice her appearance? He was angry at her. Wasn't he?

Dinah held out the basket. "We've got bread, hard tack, and cheese plus some leftover biscuits from last night's dinner. What else do you need?"

"Nothing here, but you should change your clothes. You can't go gallivanting around the prairie on a manhunt wearing a dress. Wait here, and I'll be back."

<hr>

Dinah set the basket on the ground and kneaded her hands. Nathan hated her. He'd made that clear. As she feared, their friendship was over as well as any possibility for more. How soon after they returned would he file for a divorce? Or would he talk the judge into an annulment, wiping away their marriage as if it had never happened?

But she would know it happened. In the years to come, she'd pull out the memories and relive the happy times. Times with Florence. Her small frame hurtling toward Dinah, arms outstretched and a wide smile on the child's face. Bent over her papers, tongue tucked in the corner of her mouth as the youngster concentrated on her task. Skipping across the yard, digging in the dirt when they planted the garden.

Her heart stuttered. The child would reside with her forever. As would her father. Her handsome, gentle, stubborn, brave father.

Nathan's image swam before her eyes. Grinning when he teased her, eyes sparkling when he laughed. His broad shoulders straining against his shirt when he swung a hammer, harvested the crops, or lifted Florence over his head. His jaw square and determined under his beard.

She might not leave here with more than the clothes on her back, but she would carry the memories with her no matter what. No one could take those away from her. Eventually, the sadness of her loss would go away, and she'd be able to relive her experiences without crying. Maybe.

Nearby, a horse nickered, and she blinked. Standing around mooning over things that would never be was a waste of precious time. She grabbed the basket and tucked the towel-wrapped packages into the saddlebags. She was still working when Nathan returned with a bundle of clothes and a bedroll.

"Here. Put these on. And be quick about it. The men are almost ready to leave."

She took the items from his hands, their fingers grazing. She gasped almost dropped the clothes.

His eyes widened, and he hissed a quick intake of breath. Then a frown darkened his face.

Plain and simple, he hated her, as he had every right to do. She pivoted and trotted into the house. Running into the bedroom, she slammed the door, and tossed the denim pants and cotton long-sleeved shirt onto the chair. She stripped her dress and unmentionables until only her shift remained. She slid her arms through the sleeves and buttoned the shirt to her neck then sat on the chair and poked her legs into the heavy pants. She pulled them on and frowned. Despite belonging to one of the smaller farmhands, the waistband stood inches from her waist. She shoved her feet into her boots, then clutched the excess material in one hand, and left the room.

"Mrs. Crowell, please help me."

The housekeeper turned, and her jaw dropped. "Dinah, what in the world are you wearing? That outfit isn't proper."

Face as hot as a skillet over a campfire, Dinah nodded. "I know, but Nathan said I had to change."

"He's probably right, but goodness, what would the ladies in town say?"

"Hopefully, nothing once they find out I'm doing this to look for Florence."

"Of course, child. I wasn't thinking." She opened a drawer near the sink and pulled out a thick rope. "I knew this thing would come in handy one day." She slipped the cord through the loops on Dinah's pants, cinched the material, then tied a knot. "Best I can do on short notice. I'll be praying."

"Thank you, Mrs. Crowell. For everything." Dinah embraced the woman for a quick moment then ran to the barn.

Nathan and the farmhands were all mounted, and Nathan held the reins of a riderless horse. His eyes shuttered and blank, he jerked his head toward the animal. "This one's for you."

She nodded and grabbed the traces from his fingers then climbed onto the horse. She squared her shoulders and settled into the saddle. "You may already have a plan, but do you remember there's an abandoned soddie about eight miles from here, up toward the western outskirts? He might have taken her there."

"How do you know about that place?"

"Livvy told me about it one day. We were talking about folks who'd come and gone." She shrugged and ducked her head. "Just a thought, but you're in charge."

"Yeah, I am, but I've already done some reconnaissance, and the man's tracks seem to go in that direction, so that's where we're headed."

Breathless, Dinah yanked the reins. Her horse whinnied and shook her head. She patted the mare's neck. "Sorry, girl. I'm so frightened." She glanced at Nathan whose face was an impassive mask. *Please, God, help us find our little girl, unharmed.*

She didn't deserve the Lord's help, but Nathan did. Hopefully, God would answer her prayer on his behalf.

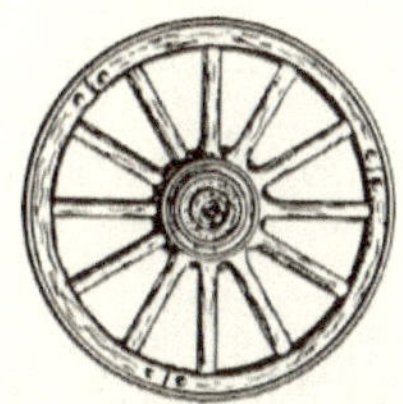

Chapter Twenty-Four

Sweat trickled between Nathan's shoulder blades and pooled under his arms in the late afternoon sun. The ball of fire might not be overhead, but its slanting rays still scorched his back. The breeze had stilled as if nature were holding its breath until the outcome of his daughter's fate. Dust clouds rose from the ground under the horses' hooves. He coughed and drew his bandanna over his nose and mouth.

He glanced at Dinah who rode beside him. Her ashen expression appeared set in stone, her porcelain skin dimmed with a light coating of dirt. Her hair was pulled into a tight bun, but tendrils of chestnut-brown hair had escaped and framed her face. Her brown eyes narrowed in a permanent squint. Ramrod straight, she gripped the reins as if her life depended on the connection. Perhaps it did.

Digging into his pocket, he retrieved a handkerchief. He held out the cloth. "Here. Wrap this around your face."

Her vacant gaze drifted toward him, and she stared at the linen. After a long moment, she nodded and reached for the cloth. She dropped the reins, letting the mare plod along while Dinah tied on the bandanna and tugged it into place. Picking up the traces, she settled into the saddle.

He blew out a sigh. How could he be so angry at the woman next to him, yet still care? Still want to ensure her safety? Still want her by his side?

Simply put, she'd lied to him when she omitted the information about her outlaw brothers. Did she think he wouldn't find out? Did she set out to deceive him, knowing that as a lawman he'd be hesitant to marry a woman with ties to a gang? What else had she lied about or failed to mention in the weeks since she'd entered their lives?

A red-tailed hawk shrieked overhead, and he startled. He watched the bird ride the air's waves, swooping and soaring in lazy arcs. Then, like a bullet from a gun, the winged creature shot toward the ground and seconds later snatched a rodent in its talons and lifted toward the cloudless sky.

He sensed rather than saw Dinah shudder. A city girl, born and bred, she probably hadn't been exposed to the circle of life. Here on the prairie, living side by side with the birds and animals brought the nature's brutality close to home.

Two hours later, Nathan spied the sod house. Three hundred yards in the distance, the grass-covered hump in the middle of a field had seen better days. The family who'd owned it vacated after one season. From what he'd heard, they'd struggled from the moment they'd arrived. First, losing a child to sickness then a drought impacted the crop, producing a poor harvest. Partway through collecting the remaining corn, a swarm of grasshoppers had appeared and wiped out what little was left. The poor man collected their meager belongings and used his proceeds to purchase a train ticket home, wherever that was.

Life was hard. No doubt about it.

He shielded his eyes and surveyed the horizon. Movement to the left of the abode. A horse. Did the animal belong to the man they were looking for, or had some squatter taken up residence? He peered at Dinah. "There's a gray pony near the house. Do you remember what the guy was riding when he came looking for the job?"

She rubbed her forehead and stared across the expanse. "No, might have been gray, but I didn't pay a lot of attention to his horse. I kept an eye on his hands and face…thought he was going to attack me again."

"Understandable." He gestured to the riders to gather, and they drew near forming a tight ring. "Someone's inside, so for now, let's assume it's our man. He'll hear our horses if we ride up, so we'll need to dismount and approach on foot. We'll surround the house. Benny, you and Zeke stay with the horses. I don't want them wandering off." He pointed to the men as he spoke. "You two take the north and south sides of the house, and you two take the front. Dinah, Jacob, and I will handle the back. Most criminals expect the posse to come at them head-on. Hopefully, by doing it this way, we've got an element of surprise. Stay as low as possible among the prairie grass. Got that?" He looked at each man, thankful to have such a stalwart and loyal crew.

Jacob held up his hand. "I'd like to pray for everyone."

Wincing, Nathan sighed. He should have thought to lead the group in prayer. He'd sent desperate pleas toward heaven during the ride to the house, but Florence had been his only concern. Shame on him for not bathing the group in prayer and asking for safety of his staff.

His foreman pulled off his Stetson and bowed his head. "Lord, thank you for leading us to this house if this is the place where Miss Florence is bein' held. Please keep her safe, and us, too, as we try to rescue her. We'd like success today, so please help us get Nathan's little girl back in his arms. We'd prefer that there be no killing, but sometimes evil has to be put down. Amen."

"Amen."

"Okay, let's do this." Nathan tugged his hat low on his forehead and slid off the horse. He grabbed the rifle from its sling and handed his pistol to Dinah. "Only use that if you can get a clean shot, and Florence is in danger."

Face taut, she nodded then crouched low beside him. Jacob huddled on the other side. Together they crept through the tall grass covering the land. Any other time of year, and they'd have nothing to hide behind. The stalks rustled as the group moved toward the house.

Nathan took a deep breath and willed his heart to beat slow and steady. He narrowed his focus on the house but listened to each sound that pricked his ears, straining to hear anything unusual to indicate the man sensed their presence or had exited the dirt structure. Sweat plastered his shirt to his back.

Time crawled. Soon they reached the clearing. He made hand gestures to Jacob and Dinah explaining they should approach from the side. They angled away from the house then crouch-walked to where he'd indicated. He slipped around the back of the structure then lowered himself to the ground and inched forward until he was under the window. He yanked off his hat and raised his head to peek in the window. *Please, God, don't let him be looking outside.*

Light from a single oil lamp provided a murky glow within the cabin. Apparently, the family who'd hightailed it home had left everything behind. A table and four chairs sat at one end of the large room. Sagging shelves held some dishes. A double bed and dresser took up the other end of the space.

Florence was tied to a chair, her face pale and tear streaked, her hair a tangled mass. Feet propped on the table, her abductor tilted back in his seat, hat pulled down over his face. His gun lay on the table. Nathan's jaw clenched, and his muscles tensed. He tightened his grip on the rifle. Relief at seeing his daughter alive and well mingled with white-hot anger at her kidnapper.

A hand squeezed his shoulder, and he dropped below the sill. Jacob put a finger to his lips. Nathan shifted so Jacob could look in the window. His foreman winked, a slow smile forming on his face. He leaned close to Nathan's ear. "I'll grab the gun; you take care of Rumpelstiltskin.

Once we've overpowered him, Dinah can come in and take care of Florence."

Nathan nodded and held up a hand to Dinah and Alfred indicating they should remain in the position. He raised three fingers then lowered them one at a time. He and Jacob rose in tandem and crept toward the door. He gripped the handle and prayed the hinges wouldn't squeal. With a curt nod, he swung open the door then rushed forward and pushed the kidnapper out of the chair. The man landed on the ground with a grunt. His hat flew off his head.

Florence screamed.

Jacob snatched the weapon from the table and pointed it at the man who scrabbled in his holster. "This what you're looking for?" He waved the pistol.

The man spat and cursed.

"Hey, none of that. We've got a young lady here." Jacob held the weapon with practiced ease.

Nathan searched the culprit and found a knife in the side of his boot. He yanked the man to his feet and pulled his arms behind him. "Dinah! Come inside."

On clattering feet, she rushed into the house and stopped. Seeing Florence, she ran to the child, untied her, and swept her into a tight embrace. Jacob grabbed the abandoned rope and tossed it to Nathan, who caught the cord one handed. In quick motions, he secured the man's wrists.

Face pressed against Dinah's shoulder, Florence whimpered.

He shoved the man toward the door. "Daylight's burning. Let's go."

Jacob nudged his shoulder. "I'll handle our…friend. You hug your daughter. I got plenty of help. We'll take care of getting this varmint to jail, even if we gotta ride all night."

"Thank you." Nathan's voice broke. His daughter was alive and unharmed. She'd probably have nightmares for a long time, but as far as he could tell, she was physically fine. "This was too easy, Jacob."

"If God be for us, who can be against us?" His foreman shrugged. "We've got a lot to be thankful for tonight."

"Amen to that."

"You boys finished congratulatin' yourselves?" The abductor glared at them, his mouth twisted into a sneer.

"Just about." Jacob poked the gun into the man's back. "Get moving."

They tramped out of the house as Nathan wrapped his arms around Dinah and his daughter. He pressed his face into the child's back, tears streaming. Dinah attempted to extricate herself from the embrace, but he held fast.

Moments passed. Reluctantly, Nathan released Dinah and his daughter. "The light is fading. As it is, we'll be riding the last hour or so in the dark. We best get going." He reached for Florence, who snuggled closer to Dinah. "I want to ride home with Mama Dinah. Is that okay?"

"Anything you want, honey."

"Anything?" Her face brightened.

He chuckled and gestured to the doorway. "Within reason."

Shoulders sagging, Dinah carried Florence outside then set her on the ground. Nibbling grass, their mounts waited nearby. Benny stood next to the animals. "Real happy everything turned out okay, boss. Mr. Muir told me it was safe to bring you the horses." He touched the brim of his hat. "Hello, Miss Florence."

"Well done, Benny. We're heading back now. I'd appreciate it if you'd remain close by us. I don't anticipate any more trouble, but you never know."

"Yes, sir."

Dinah climbed on her horse, and Nathan handed Florence up to her. Their fingers brushed, and the now familiar jolt shot down his arms. Against his better judgment, he'd fallen in love with this beautiful, tenacious, and frustrating woman. He had it bad, and that wasn't good. Could he build a marriage with a woman who'd deceived him to the detriment of his daughter, his only child?

He shook his head, shoved his foot into the stirrup, then swung his leg over the horse. They headed toward home, and he watched his daughter and Dinah through his peripheral vision. Florence was snuggled against the woman's chest, thumb in her mouth and eyes closed, seemingly asleep. Dinah held the reins in one hand, her other arm wrapped tightly around the child. Dinah's back was stiff as a board and her gaze riveted on their destination; her lips moved quietly. Was she praying or talking to Florence?

Mesmerized by her profile in the growing darkness, he continued to stare. He'd be a fool to hold her brothers' actions against her. She'd proven her mettle time and again, especially tonight, riding into danger, head held high. Other than withholding the information about her family, she'd done nothing wrong. The Bloody Tubs didn't allow female members, so she wouldn't have had anything to do with them or their nefarious actions. He couldn't continue to blame her for deeds she hadn't committed.

He sighed. Would she forgive him for the things he'd said to her? Or would she call it quits and file for a divorce? His heart fell. He'd done a poor job of trying to woo her, so the latter seemed the most likely prospect.

Dinah's Dilemma

Chapter Twenty-Five

Sunlight streamed through the window, and a light breeze fluttered the curtains. Dinah stared out the glass. After sobbing into her pillow last night, she'd slept like the dead then awakened with a throbbing headache. A glance in the mirror had confirmed she looked as awful as she felt. Swollen eyes and a blotchy face stared back at her before she moved away from her reflection.

Outside, the farmhands went about their work as if they hadn't been involved in a life-and-death rescue the previous day. The fragrant aroma of bacon permeated the room indicating Mrs. Crowell's presence in the kitchen. Florence's high-pitched tones were muffled behind the door.

Dinah blew out a loud breath. She's miss this place, but leaving was for the best. Wreaking havoc from the moment she arrived, she'd upended the entire farm. Nathan deserved a woman above reproach, and her behavior had not come close. Seeking forgiveness from God, she prayed all the way home from the sod house. He'd cleansed her, and her sins were as far from the east is from the west as the Bible said, but absolution didn't mean there weren't consequences.

Nathan would be hard pressed to forgive and forget. Her deceit, coupled with her brothers' actions that lead to the death of his wife, were more than a man could be expected to excuse. Besides, he still loved Georgianna, and she would always be part of their marriage.

Florence giggled, and Dinah's eyes welled with tears. The child had opened her heart to Dinah, accepting her without question, allowing her to become her new mama, a role she'd never considered. She wanted to keep in touch with letters, but correspondence would confuse the situation. The little girl wouldn't understand why Dinah had to leave, so it was better to sever the relationship. Florence was young enough that the summer of 1870 would eventually fade from memory.

Dinah moved to the dresser, pulled out her belongings, and filled her bag. Where to go? Maryland was not an option. But perhaps Boston might be a good location. Would Mrs. Crenshaw understand when Dinah spilled all that had occurred in Nebraska? Would the widow be willing to try placing her again? Or had she used up her last second chance?

Foregoing the items Nathan purchased for her, the satchel was soon packed. She picked up her Bible, placed it on top of her clothes, and closed the latch. She'd leave her books for Florence…and Nathan's new bride…if he chose one. Opening the drawer in the nightstand, she withdrew a pencil and sheet of paper, a precious commodity, but necessary if she was going to slip out unnoticed.

Sitting in the chair, she tapped the pencil on her thigh. What to write? How to capture her thoughts without casting blame or sounding like she was justifying her conduct? Should she tell Nathan she loved him? No, he should never know her true feelings. With few words, she indicated that she was leaving, and he was welcome to seek an annulment of their marriage. He should not look for her, and she wished him the very best.

She folded the letter, wrote his name on the back, and propped the sheet against the oil lamp. Satisfied she'd done all she could, she pushed up the casement wide enough for her body, tossed her bag to the ground, and climbed over the sill. She smoothed her skirts and picked up her satchel. Marching over the uneven ground, she headed for the barn. With any luck one of the boys would be there, and she could ask him to drive her to the train station. Otherwise, she'd borrow a horse then make arrangements for the animal to be returned. Perhaps that was a better solution than getting one of the hands in trouble.

The barn smelled of fresh hay, manure, leather, and animals, a scent she'd grown to appreciate and associate with good memories. Heart pounding, she walked among the stalls. Were all the horses in use? Would she have to walk to the train station? Her shoulders slumped. Maybe she should wait until nightfall, then no one would know she'd left until morning. Indecisive, she shuffled her feet and shifted her bag from one hand to the other.

Nathan appeared from one of the enclosures. "Dinah? What are you doing with your bag?"

She whirled and rushed from the barn, her satchel hitting her leg with every step.

"Dinah, wait!" Footsteps thundered as he ran to catch up with her. He grabbed her shoulder, stopping her progress. He turned her toward him, myriad emotions on his face. "Are you leaving? Where are you going?"

"I have to go." Her chin trembled. "I can't stay. It's not fair to you or Florence. Or me."

"I don't understand."

"You don't?" She let go of the bag and fisted her hands on her hip. "You made your feelings clear before we left to rescue Florence. You hate me. I've done nothing but lie to you, and my actions caused terrible things to happen. Praise God, Florence is safe, but we can't continue in this manner. I didn't mean for things to get so convoluted. I just wanted to find some happiness, away from my brothers and stepfather and their machinations. Carve out some slice of life that didn't involve wondering when I'd see a report in the newspaper of something they'd done or open the door to a police officer or be shunned because polite society looked down on my family." Tears coursed down her cheeks, and she swiped them away. Why did she have to cry? Now, he'd not only hate her, he'd pity her. "I have to go. I can't continue to live a lie."

His eyes widened. "But you're not. I know everything." He reached for her then dropped his hands. "Don't I?"

She wrapped her arms around her middle and bowed her head. She couldn't look at him. He'd see what was in her heart.

With a gentle touch, he lifted her chin until her eyes met his. "Tell me. I promise not to get angry. Please."

Was that compassion in his gaze? Her face reddened. How would he react when she blurted out her feelings? Her chest tightened. She should have headed down the lane on foot and avoided any sort of confrontation.

"Dinah, I can see you arguing with yourself. Unless you've killed a man, nothing you tell me will be a shock."

"I love you." There, she'd said it. No turning back. "I love you, and I don't want to keep it secret anymore, so I have to leave. I can't see you every day knowing I have feelings for you. Wifely feelings."

His jaw dropped. "You love me?"

"Yes." Her voice squeaked. How pathetic. "I don't want to put you in a difficult position, so I need to go."

"What sort of difficult position?" Confusion clouded his expression. "Why do you think you can't tell me how you feel? We're married."

"Because you still love Georgianna and not me." Her chin trembled, and she pressed her lips together. Why couldn't she control her emotions?

Nathan chuckled, his face lighting up the dim interior of the barn. "What—?

He pulled her to him and kissed her, his lips searching and tentative at first, then more insistent. She melted against him, her arms slipping around his waist. Her heart pounded in her ears, blocking out all other sound.

Releasing her, he pressed a kiss on her forehead. "Oh, Dinah, my poor bride. I'm so sorry you felt you needed to hold your feelings inside. We haven't been married long, and I'm already making a mess of things. You see, darling, I love you, too, but I didn't tell you, and I almost lost you." He raked his fingers through his hair. "Last night on the ride home, watching you, I realized that I don't care about anyone else in your life. Yes, your brothers did a terrible thing, but Georgianna's death isn't your fault. Can never be your fault." He blew out a loud sigh. "I should have come to you first thing this morning to speak with you."

"But you still love her, don't you?"

"Listen carefully." He stroked her jaw with his thumb. "Yes, I love Georgianna. We had a good marriage, and she holds a place in my heart. She's the mother of my child, but she's gone. My heart is big enough for more love, love for you, Dinah, and I was a fool not to tell you. Please stay. Please be my wife. For real."

Dinah's breath caught. Nathan loved her. "Oh, Nathan—"

"Mama Dinah, where are you going?" Florence tugged on her skirt.

When had she crept up on them? Dinah looked down at the youngster then back at Nathan. Her heart swelled. "I'm not going anywhere, sweetheart. I'm staying right here."

Nathan picked her up and swung her around. "Wahoo!" He set her on her feet and showered kisses on her face then dropped to one knee and cradled her hands in his. "Dinah, will you please marry me." He cocked his head and winked. "Again."

"I'd be honored to be your wife."

Dinah's Dilemma

August, 1871

Chapter Twenty-Six

Baby Georgianna wailed, and Dinah picked up her three-month-old daughter. Florence rushed to her side and patted the sobbing child. "She cries a lot, Mama."

Across the room, Nathan laughed. "So did you at her age. Crying is what babies do."

Florence crossed her arms. "Then I don't think I want one."

"That will change, sweetheart." Dinah ruffled Florence's hair then glanced at her stepfather sitting next to Nathan. "You look tired, Father. Are you feeling ill?"

He shook his head. "No, just getting used to backbreaking work. This husband of yours is a taskmaster." He winked at Dinah. "But I'm grateful for what he's done. Taking in an old reprobate like me. He's a good man."

"Yes, he is." She cuddled the infant close and kissed her head. "And how are you faring, Mother?"

Seated near the fireplace, Dinah's mother stopped mending the shirt in her hands. "Just fine. I thought I'd miss the excitement of living in the city, but I don't. I couldn't be happier, living here with all of you, being part of your lives." She sniffled. "And the church people have been loving and welcoming."

Nathan smiled. "They're a wonderful bunch. And the way Lincoln is growing, you'll have your city soon enough."

Dinah's father held up his hands as if in surrender. "You can keep your city. Too many temptations. God has changed me, but I still have days where the desire to gamble threatens to overtake me." He poked Nathan. "Then this man intervenes and puts me to work making me too tired to head to the tables in town."

"Whatever it takes." Nathan clapped him on the shoulder.

Her stepfather laughed then sobered. "Thank you for making my stepdaughter so happy, and for granting your forgiveness to my boys. They'll be in prison for a long time, but perhaps they will consider their actions."

"Prison can hold many forms, sir." Nathan sighed. "Your boys are behind bars in a physical prison, but I was trapped in a prison of my own doing, clinging to my grief and anger. Who am I to judge?"

"I guess my gambling problems are a prison as well, and I appreciate all you've done to set me free."

"Not me, sir. Your freedom came from the Lord. I'm just a fellow traveler."

"Well, I'm glad to have you along for the journey."

Dinah's heart swelled. The road had been rough, but her family had come to a place of healing. *Thank You, God.*

THE END

What did you think of *Dinah's Dilemma?*

Thank you so much for purchasing *Dinah's Dilemma*. You could have selected any number of books to read, but you chose this book.

I hope it added encouragement and exhortation to your life. If so, it would be nice if you could share this book with your family and friends by posting to Facebook (www.facebook.com) and/or Twitter (www.twitter.com).

If you enjoyed this book and found some benefit in reading it, I'd appreciate it if you could take some time to post a review on Amazon, Goodreads, Kobo, GooglePlay, Apple Books, or other book review site of your choice. Your feedback and support will help me to improve my writing craft for future projects and make this book even better.
Thank you again for your purchase.

Blessings,
Linda Shenton Matchett

Dinah's Dilemma

Acknowledgments

Although writing a book is a solitary task, it is not a solitary journey. There have been many who have helped and encouraged me along the way.

My parents, Richard and Jean Shenton, who presented me with my first writing tablet and encouraged me to capture my imagination with words. Thanks, Mom and Dad!

Scribes212 – my ACFW online critique group: Valerie Goree, Marcia Lahti, and the late Loretta Boyett (passed on to Glory, but never forgotten). Without your input, my writing would not be nearly as effective.

Eva Marie Everson – my mentor/instructor with Christian Writers' Guild. You took a timid, untrained student and turned her into a writer. Many thanks!

SincNE, and the folks who coordinate the Crimebake Writing Conference. I have attended many writing conferences, but without a doubt, Crimebake is one of the best. The workshops, seminars, panels, critiques, and every tiny aspect are well-executed, professional, and educational.

Special thanks to Hank Phillippi Ryan, Halle Ephron, and Roberta Isleib for your encouragement and spot-on critiques of my work.

Significant thanks go to Viola Shenton, my father's wife, who gave me the idea to use Dad's family genealogy for characters' names and then spent several hours with me scouring the databases. Thanks, Vi!

Additional thanks to Mike Remiger, a retired farmer from Minnesota who spoke with me at length about farming and ranching in the midwest, with specific information about Nebraska. He has a wealth of knowledge, and I hope my story honors him and his family as well as all the men and women whose backbreaking dedication feeds this country. Any errors are mine alone.

Thanks to my Book Brigade who provide information, encouragement, and support.

Paula Proofreader (https://paulaproofreader.wixsite.com/home): I'm so glad I found you! My work is cleaner because of your eagle eye. Any mistakes are completely mine.

A heartfelt thank you to my brothers, Jack Shenton and Douglas Shenton, and my sister, Susan Shenton Greger for being enthusiastic cheerleaders during my writing journey. Your support means more than you'll know.

My husband, Wes, deserves special kudos for understanding my need to write. Thank you for creating my writing room – it's perfect, and I'm thankful for it every day. Thank you for your willingness to accept a house that's a bit cluttered, laundry that's not always done, and meals on the go. I love you.

And finally, to God be the glory. I thank Him for giving me the gift of writing and the inspiration to tell stories that shine the light on His goodness and mercy.

Be sure to read the next story in the *Westward Home and Hearts Mail Order Bride series!*

Hannah's Hardship by Marie Higgins

Hannah Ross wants only one thing – to leave her rotten home town where the gossipmongers won't stop spreading rumors and to start a new life. Becoming a mail-order bride is the only way. Of course, she must make her new husband believe she was widowed. How else could she explain the baby growing inside her belly? Trying to put her disastrous past behind her, she mustn't let anyone know the truth about her pregnancy.

Want more romance from author Linda Shenton Matchett?

Read on for the first chapter in *Love's Harvest*, book one in the "Wartime Brides" series.

Volga Region, Russia, 1923

"We'll die if we don't leave this place. Pack only what you can carry." Edmund Hirsch poked his bony arms into the sleeves of his wool coat that sported more holes than Swiss cheese. A paroxysm of coughing gripped his body, the result of a mustard gas attack on his German platoon nine years ago during The Great War.

After several minutes the coughing ceased, and he mopped the sweat from his forehead with a dingy, gray handkerchief. "Be ready. We set out tomorrow at first light."

"Where will we go, *Vati*?" Five-year-old Conrad's voice trembled.

"Don't be a baby, Conrad." Older by two minutes, Conrad's twin brother, Manfred, finished tying his boot laces and jumped off the chair, his shoes clomping against the bare wood floor. His bright blue eyes blazed above his hollow cheeks.

"Hush, children." Noreen stroked Conrad's white-blond hair and met her husband's terse look with one of her own. "You heard your father. There's no time to waste."

━━━ ⬤ ━━━

Noreen yanked the zipper closed on her over-stuffed canvas satchel. Always resourceful, Edmund had attached straps to the moss-green bag so she could wear it on her back. She would also carry a suitcase in each hand. The journey promised to be arduous.

Sighing, she wiped a weary hand across her dry eyes. Even if she had any tears remaining, crying was useless. It would not make their situation less dire.

Muted voices and the occasional bump filtered through the ceiling from the boys' bedroom above. Noreen shivered and hunched into her threadbare, ruby-red sweater. An impulse purchase made during her honeymoon, the garment held more memories than warmth. Edmund insisted it brought out the roses in her cheeks.

She tossed the bulging satchel to the floor and turned her attention to the yawning luggage on the bed. Two steel pots and a fry pan nestled in the bottom of one boxy, brown suitcase between faded blue towels that had been a belated wedding present from her mother and father.

Hopefully, Edmund would find somewhere they could live in his home country with enough food to actually cook. Here, along the Volga River in Russia, the crops had failed again, and the famine was entering its second year. The decision whether to eat or plant their seed wheat had caused many families to die of starvation.

Shuffling footsteps sounded behind her. She turned as Edmund enveloped her in his arms. Nestling against his too-thin chest, she breathed in his musky scent. He bent and kissed her forehead, his black beard scraping her skin.

"You work too hard." He tucked a stray strand of her nutmeg-colored hair behind her ear.

She leaned into his touch. "Isn't that why you married me?"

"No, *Schatzi,* it is most certainly not." He grinned. "You stole my heart. I had to marry you, or I would die a broken man."

"Don't joke about that. Our friends are dying every day." She frowned. "Who knew this famine would last so long? If it weren't for the bit of help arriving from America's Volga Relief Society, matters would be much worse."

"They are sending more assistance than we are receiving. Jakob told me there is proof the government is confiscating some of the packages and keeping the money to construct new buildings and conduct repairs. As always, development of the country is valued above the lives of the people."

"Shhh!" She pressed the work-worn fingers of her right hand against his lips. "You could get in trouble for saying that. Then where would we be?"

Edmund hugged her. "There is no one to hear us, but I understand your fear. Many unexplained disappearances make for extreme caution." He released her and gestured toward the pile of clothes on their bed. "Enough depressing talk. What can I do to help?"

"Do you have our passports? With the government ratcheting up the price, we have no more savings to purchase new ones."

"Now who's speaking out against the authorities?" He patted the breast pocket of his coat. "I have the passports and our traveling papers safe and sound."

"Good." Noreen waved him away. "Then go see what the boys are about. I gave explicit instructions about what to pack, but they have a mind of their own." She shook her head. "Well, Manfred does. Conrad simply tags along."

He kissed the tip of her nose and raised his hand in mock salute. "*Jawohl!*"

She giggled and pushed him out of the room. Closing the door behind him, she sobered and dropped to her knees next to the bed. "Dear Heavenly Father, thank You for Edmund. He is a good man. Give him strength for the journey and keep us safe as we travel. Soften the hearts of his family so they will welcome us home."

Home.

Berlin was Edmund's home. Not hers.

English born and bred, Noreen stroked the floral bedspread as visions of daffodils in Regents Park flitted through her head, their golden yellow blooms swaying in the breeze. Big Ben soaring into the sky. Tower Bridge spanning the River Thames. Pristine white swans fishing the waters of Serpentine Lake in Hyde Park where a chance meeting changed the trajectory of her life.

In an effort to heal his damaged lungs, Edmund moved to London after the war. Someone told him the damp English air would act as a balm. A lover of art, he had attended the Spring Festival where she sat under a tent selling her baskets.

She climbed to her feet, and her gaze sought out the willow basket on their dresser. The basket Edmund purchased when he returned to her booth after taking his girlfriend home. His last date with the woman.

Noreen's smile broadened. Who knew basket weaving would catch her a husband? She flushed as she remembered the conversation.

"If I purchase this basket, will you go out with me?"

"What about your girlfriend?"

"I told her we were finished, that I was going to marry you."

"Isn't that a bit rash? You don't even know me."

"I know enough."

After a whirlwind courtship, Edmund asked for her hand in marriage. Her parents objected, so Edmund took her to the register office where he wed her in front of two gray-haired, bored-looking clerks. A year later the twins were born, and her parents decided being grandparents was more important than holding a grudge. They eventually grew to love their German son-in-law as much as their daughter did. Enough to support the family's move to Russia in another effort to heal Edmund's lungs. She swallowed against the lump in her throat. Her parents' death last year in a train accident still stung.

Overheard, a thump followed by laughter broke her reverie. Warmth filled her. She loved her country, but she loved Edmund more. That is why she would leave all but her most necessary possessions and travel to yet another foreign country to live with her in-laws. People she had never met who spoke a language she didn't know.

Other Titles
Romance

Love's Harvest, Wartime Brides, Book 1

Love's Rescue, Wartime Brides, Book 2

Love's Belief, Wartime Brides, Book 3

Love's Allegiance, Wartime Brides, Book 4

Love Found in Sherwood Forest

A Love Not Forgotten

On the Rails

A Doctor in the House (The Hope of Christmas Collection)

Spies & Sweethearts, Sisters in Service, Book 1

The Mechanic & the MD, Sisters in Service, Book 2

The Widow & the War Correspondent, Sisters in Service, Book 3

Mystery
Under Fire, Ruth Brown Mystery Series, Book 1

Under Ground, Ruth Brown Mystery Series, Book 2

Under Cover, Ruth Brown Mystery Series, Book 3

Murder of Convenience, Women of Courage, Book 1

Murder at Madison Square Garden, Women of Courage, Book 2

Non-Fiction
WWII Word Find, Volume 1

Biography

Linda Shenton Matchett writes about ordinary people who did extraordinary things in days gone by. She is a volunteer docent and archivist at the Wright Museum of WWII and a trustee for her local public library. Born in Baltimore, Maryland, a stone's throw from Fort McHenry, she has lived in historical places most of her life. Now located in central New Hampshire, Linda's favorite activities include exploring historic sites and immersing herself in the imaginary worlds created by other authors.

Website/blog: http://www.LindaShentonMatchett.com
Facebook: http://www.facebook.com/LindaShentonMatchettAuthor
Pinterest: http://www.pinterest.com/lindasmatchett
Amazon: https://www.amazon.com/Linda-Shenton-Matchett/e/B01DNB54S0
Goodreads: http://www.goodreads.com/author_linda_matchett
Bookbub: http://www.bookbub.com/authors/linda-shenton-matchett

Dinah's Dilemma